RISE OF THE SONS OF DARKNESS

THE TRUTH ABOUT THE DARK

To: Jenny, Mike, Blake, + Madelay
Thanks for your hospitality
Love you Guys

R Battle

ROB BATTLE

outskirts
press

Outskirts Press, Inc.
http://www.outskirtspress.com

ISBN: 978-1-9772-1096-8

Library of Congress Control Number: 2019905124

Outskirts Press and the "OP" logo are trademarks belonging to Outskirts Press, Inc.

PRINTED IN THE UNITED STATES OF AMERICA

PART 1
Zarian: Keeper of the Sharuk

N o one remembered how the war started. Even the oldest of vampires were unable to recall who or what caused the events. No documentation detailed what led to every race of vampires taking up arms, everywhere around the vampire world.

Before the war, there was an epidemic of vampires vanishing without a trace. Panic spread from village to village as loved ones disappeared. Even the mightiest of vampire kingdoms with their high walls, barricades, and guards were not enough to keep them safe.

Talk circulated that a natural phenomenon that affected vampires caused the event. Lightning flashes piercing through vampire domiciles and solar flares at night were some of the rumors. There was no evidence of a natural disaster. There was no proof of a supernatural event that could have caused so many vampires to disappear. The fear intensified when the crisis was believed to be caused by biological warfare. Though there was no proof of a biological attack, the fires of fear grew hotter, and war was declared.

The first year of war became ten years of fear and blame. Ten years of war became hundreds of years of destruction, hatred, and fear. The conflict between the many vampire clans continued for over a thousand years; each day was more vicious than the last. The devastation caused by the war became more extreme as time went on.

The lush green fields and mountains were now barren waste-lands. The velvet black sky that once glistened with stars was now scarred with pollution. Moonlight rarely pierced the blanket of smog.

Weapons of mass destruction destroyed entire vampire colonies. Vampire kingdoms rose and fell throughout the war. Cultures and beliefs vanished, while entire races and species were executed. The vampire world started to decay and die. Still, the war carried on.

The Kingdoms of the Drak and the Vlad were the only two realms that reigned at the beginning of the war and continued to stand. The Vlad were well dressed and well-spoken but were merciless killers taught from birth. The Drak were always tactical and practical and followed the philosophy of "work smarter, not harder."

The hatred between the two clans made their battles even more ferocious. Soldiers from both kingdoms were in the heat of battle when both sides, frozen with fear, stopped fighting. Word of the cease in combat was sent out to both kingdoms. The kings mounted their horses, and soon both were en route to the scene of battle. The two kings looked across the battlefield and saw each other. Between them was a river of blood that flowed down the mountain.

The sight of the blood river was the moment the war ended. Word of the event circulated the vampire world. Within days the fighting had stopped everywhere.

After the war, the realization of the amount of devastation to the vampire world was starting to take form.

Negotiations of territories started, and the Congregation Council was established. The Congregation Council became a check and balance between the last of the two kingdoms. Bordering colonies between the two kingdoms were set as boundaries to keep the realm separated. These colonies were established as a neutral zone to be governed by the Congregation Council.

After the Congregation Council's establishment, it was decided by all that there should be an archive of the vampire lineage. Historical data was collected on the race, cultures, and species of vampires that no longer existed. Hopefully, they would never be forgotten.

The Congregation Council established libraries as a place to learn about other cultures of the vampire world, in hopes of preventing another world war. These libraries were placed throughout the vampire world, to include the two kingdoms. The libraries in each realm were designed to be emergency backup computer servers. The library headquarters was called the Master Library. The Master Library was built in Midland. Midland was a village created to be the point of equal distance between the Kingdom of the Vlad and the Kingdom of the Drak.

The Master Library created an archive of all vampires living and dead. This archive was a living document that established a census of every type of vampire; this archive was called the Sharuk. The Sharuk included a network of communication between various library branches, which kept the Sharuk current.

A common trait amongst all vampires was the ability to adapt; after all, we were predators. The war caused significant changes in our everyday life. Our domiciles were built inside mountains, underground, or created with reinforced walls, due to the potential of bomb attacks or worse. The war caused the vampire world to leap forward in technology. Computer technology was created at least one hundred years before humans. Computer programs were useful in making everyday life easier to manage, especially when life revolved around the night.

The Sharuk documented the past and current lives of vampires in real time. If a vampire was born, created, or died it would show up on the Sharuk within minutes of the event. The Sharuk was created and maintained by historiographers in the libraries. We were called the Keepers; our task was to archive the vampire world and keep the Sharuk updated.

My name is Zarian Kane; when I was born, I was sent to the library orphanage. At the orphanage, I was put in a position to be a Keeper and lived in the library until I was old enough to have a domicile of my own. Becoming a Keeper was not a job of choice. Most vampires born with mental or physical disabilities were placed in a specific position in society; others were not so lucky.

I was considered lucky. For the past 205 years, I have been a Keeper. My left arm was thin, with a slight bow shape from the forearm to my hand. My left arm was proportionally smaller than my right. The fingers on my left hand formed into one solid appendage.

My skin was the color of creamy milk chocolate. My eyes—or better stated my pupils—were brown hazel. I was short, about five feet five inches tall on a good day. Some would say I had a scrawny-thin build like a malnourished teenage boy. I prefer to think of myself as slender and sleek. In general, I was nothing like the image most would perceive as a predator of the night. Although I hunched over slightly and walked with a limp, the limitations of my disability were not severe enough to prevent me from becoming a Keeper. Those of us that were severely physically or mentally disabled, or later became so, could not be Keepers and were destroyed.

As a child, I spent many nights sitting on my bed wondering why I was selected to live, and others were not. As far back as I could remember, I considered my arm an appendage that was not a part of me. This appendage stole my good arm and took its place; it was an enemy that I had to learn to live with.

When I was a little older, fifty or sixty years later, I started treating my appendage as an associate. Every so often I called it Fran. Fran was an associate that was not quite a close enough to be called friend, so Fran seemed to fit. Although I had a small hunch and walked with a limp, these physical traits were not my focus.

There were times when I took my lunch break and read some of the greats in vampire literature. A patron would walk up and ask if there were any Keepers around to help find a specific book. I would stand and offer my assistance. That was when the look of surprise followed by disgust crossed their face.

I would sadly look down at Fran. "Without you, I would look normal," I murmured.

I never knew my parents. I was taken away immediately after my birth. For about 195 years, Professor Jeremiah was my caretaker, mentor, and friend. No one knew how old the professor was, but he had been around for a while. Some say the professor was the first vampire with a disability to live. The professor may no longer be my caretaker, but he will always be my mentor and friend. Sometimes I feel he is much more; he knows me more than I know myself.

He walked toward me with that look on his face. That look that said, *why are you letting the worthless dictate your worth?*

His walk was always slow and deliberate; his crutches glided silently across the floor. His hair was tousled and messy, but his eyes were focused on me for the entire journey across the room. A small smile lightened the weight of his gaze on his last few steps toward me.

"Making new friends?" he said, sitting across from me.

The professor took out his pipe and put it in his mouth, and my head shrunk between my shoulders. It wasn't that I did not like the smell of smoke; the professor never lit his pipe. When he took it out, it was widely perceived by all who knew him that he was about to say something substantial and profound, and sometimes long-winded.

"They are like buzzards, ya know. They squawk, they swoop down at you, they may even peck at you. When you lay there and take it—let them get to you—that's when you are dead." He emphasized his point by leaning forward in his chair, taking the pipe from his mouth. "That's when they can get to the important part of you, and they will do it without a fight. Don't let them! Don't let them get to you, my young friend. Their words have strength only when you give it to them."

The professor got up and walked away. He never waited for a response. Immediate responses meant you had not contemplated his words and processed their meaning. Like most of his tests, you were evaluated by the way you performed, not by what you said.

I thought on his words and all the times he called me "young friend." Deep down, I knew I was more than a friend. He was the only father figure I had ever known. Although it was never said, I knew I was one of his favorites.

The professor was a very old vampire. It was believed that he was the first vampire with a disability. After the war ended, the professor came out of hiding and was influential in the agreement to use our kind as Keepers. How he managed that was a miracle, but the wonder went only so far. Some of the more severely challenged vampires were still executed for being a potential burden.

The process to prove that we were vampires too and we deserved the same rights as everyone else was long and hard. There were a few hundred of us now, including the youngsters still in the library orphanage. Our goal was to show we were an essential part of society and hoped to be treated as such. We wanted to be kept with our families and allowed to have families of our own.

Those dreams of equality were attainable, but it was difficult when the ones oppressing us would not die off or evolve. Optimistically, it had been only 365 years since the library's establishment. To a vampire that seemed like yesterday; until then, we patiently waited for our time to come.

I went back to work, feeling confused. I was sad and hopeful, contemplating the future of my kind. I sat at my computer and continued to input data from the Sharuk into the Sharuk program. There were so many different vampires in the world; I wondered if they had been treated as equals. Then again, I guess they were not, or some of them would not be extinct or nearly wiped out of existence. I hoped that by putting as much detail about them as possible in the Sharuk, I was honoring them.

One month ago, I was in the process of putting data in the Sharuk into our new historical program; we were systematically updating the Sharuk digital format. As a student of computer technology, I felt retrieving information from the Sharuk would be functional with this new system software.

As my colleagues traveled different parts of the vampire world in search of new data to keep the Sharuk up to date, the traveling Keepers discovered discrepancies in the program. At first, they thought that a human had hacked into the system.

Theoretically, that was impossible; the human would have to use a vampires' computer. Humans do not have the telepathic ability to get into our computer systems. Humans could not translate the vampire script on our keyboards. As another security measure, only a creature bred from a vampire could read a vampire's screen.

We deduced that a vampire was trying to hack into the Sharuk's program, but why? We decided to trace the link back to the vampire hacker, but their telepathic lockout was too strong. We concluded the intruder was of a very powerful bloodline. The Congregation Council, the vampire law of the land, was notified.

A few days had passed, and I heard a knock on my door just before dawn; it was two uniformed men. I was visited by the Enforcers of the Order and Law, Enthol for short. The Enthol are composed of half-hybrids—vampires that are part human. One of the many talents of the Enthol was to hunt the vampires that put our race in danger. Some vampires went out into the human world and hunted humans for sport or needless killings. The Enthols found and returned these rogue vampires and brought them before the Congregation Council for justice. Now they were at my door.

"Could you please step outside, sir?" the Enthol closest to me requested. Since vampires don't tan, I could assume that he was bi-racial. From his thin, toned build, he looked to be a first generation. Since he was a first-generation half-hybrid, genetically he was powerful and fast, possibly as strong and fast as a regular vampire.

"Zarian Kane, you have been charged with the theft of the Sharuk to bring to the humans and exploit our existence. Our sources report that you were seen with a printed copy of the Sharuk," said the other Enthol.

He was very muscular, which is not in the general genetics of a vampire. I would say he was second or third generation.

"But I didn't take it. Who has told you these lies?" I was appalled.

"That's not your concern! What is your concern, is you have until the next nightfall to return it to the Temple of the Congregation Council, or you will watch the sunrise!" the first Enthol threatened.

A s I walked back inside, the phone rang. I picked it up and heard heavy breathing on the line. "Hello, who's there?" I asked, channeling the fear of whoever was on the other side.

"Zarian listen to me. We have never met, but we are both kindred Keepers. You are in danger! We all are in danger. We were close to finding the hacker when the Enthol came in and accused us of stealing information out of the Sharuk. Oh, God, they found me! You must leave before you are trapped in the dawn and can't escape! Our combined findings are in the Sharuk computer program. We must band together if we are to survive. Remember, we are still vampires, no matter what we look like."

"Who is this?" I asked. "How did you get my number?"

"There's no time for this. The answer is in the sys—"

A piercing scream came through the phone — the sound of a man being beaten and tortured echoed in my ear. The sound of someone begging for mercy. I also heard the men in the background laughing.

I hung up the phone and frantically ran to the bedroom. I made a sharp turn into the doorway and banged my hip on the corner of my dresser. The impact caused me to spin and flop clumsily onto my bed.

"Why me?" I grunted while rocking back and forth on the bed, trying to wish the pain away faster.

I reached under the bed and found an old duffel bag.

I tossed the bag on the bed and fumbling through my dressers.

I stuffed a few items of clothes in the bag, and started to think of where to go in less than an hour. I thought, *why am I packing? Even if I get out of here tonight, I can't survive out there; I have never been out of the confines of the village.* I could not worry about that; I had to flee. I grabbed my things and head out the door. I looked around; the streets were empty, and for a good reason. The night sky was showing faint hints of purple which meant sunrise would be soon—real soon.

I ran as fast as I could to the end of the block.

"I must go further!" I said to myself as I reached another block.

I started to feel the burn deep inside as I reached the end of the street. Sweating and panting, I cursed myself for being out of shape. The burning became more intense, and I knew that the physical exertion from running was not the cause. It was my body having what was sometimes called a supernatural allergic reaction to the sun.

I had never been outside this close to sunrise. It felt like my soul was on fire and I was being torched from the inside out. It was getting hotter and hotter. It was too far to go back home.

The rays of the sun peeked through the trees in the distance. The hue of the purple-colored clouds began to show signs of orange. The air all around was getting thicker with each breath. The pain was great; I could hardly move. I crumbled to my knees, trying to hold back my screams.

"What's this? A utility hole cover, thank the gods." I moaned as I pulled open the lid and climbed inside. As I closed the top, sun rays shot through the cracks and burned my fingers. I lost my grip and plummeted some 20 feet to the bottom of the ladder. I braced myself for the upcoming thud. The thud as I hit bottom came after a short splash. There were a few inches of water at the bottom of the ladder— not nearly enough to break my fall.

The water at the bottom may have been filthy, but it helped to soothe my burning flesh. I felt weak, but I needed to move on—but to where? I had never been away from the sanctuary of my village.

The tunnel was dark. The darkness of the tunnel felt both scary and safe. I was not afraid of the dark; I was scared of what lurked in the dark. I felt safe down here, at least for the moment, because there was no more painful sunlight.

There was a sidewalk or a hardscape surface along the wall of the sewage tunnel. My eyes adjusted to the darkness of this human-made cave. I had no idea where I was. I did not know where I was going.

I walked until my legs began to cramp. I found a dry area in a corner in the long, dark tunnel and stopped to rest. I heard something moving in the distance. It was getting closer.

"They found me," I whispered to myself. I tried to be still as possible.

They won't take me; I won't let them, I thought.

The noise was upon me. To my relief, the sound was not the Enthol. The loud sloshing through the darkness was a human. He stumbled and grunted as he made his way down the tunnel. There was a light of some sort in his hand, but he did not seem to be using it.

From the look and smell of the human, he had been in the sewer for a while. The human seemed to know where he was going and sang merrily on his way. His voice had a high pitch as he sang about dunken swaylors earl layed in da mourning.

I felt my fangs come out for the first time. I must feed, and this poor wandering soul would be my first victim. I leaped out at the man as if I were a comic book Dracula. The man clobbered me over the head with a bottle. I didn't quite see stars, but there was a flash of white light on impact.

A small gash opened on my forehead, just above my hairline. I felt the stinging of the alcohol dripping down the cut of my freshly wounded head. I fell backward and watched him stumble away. He did not yell or scream. The human casually stumbled off into the dark.

Surprisingly, I shook the blow off and tackled him in one swift leap. I pulled him close with my dominant arm and held him with my less physical arm. I pressed my fangs into his neck, and I felt the rush of his blood course through the tubes in my fangs and out the opening in the back of my throat.

In my mind, I said, "I only want enough to survive," but something came over me. I couldn't stop myself.

The next thing I knew he was dead, murdered by my hands. I felt remorseful yet extremely powerful as I stood over his limp body. The power I felt made me feel guilty for sacrificing this human for my own selfish needs.

"I am sorry. I appreciate your sacrifices" I said as I bowed to the lifeless body.

I continued my journey through the murky water of the sewage tunnel until I reached a fork.

There was a lump on my head, but the bleeding had stopped. My charred fingers stung a little and were only slightly discolored. My back was achy, and my legs were cramping. I needed to stop.

"I need to stop and rest," I said to myself as I cleared away some debris to make a place to rest. The goal was to catch my breath for a few minutes and think of a plan.

I fell asleep. Hours passed, but lying on the hard, wet concrete, it felt like days. My body was achy and stiff from sleeping on the floor, but my burns and wounds were all healed.

It was still dark here in the tunnel. There was no hint of sunlight anywhere. I had a sense the sun was starting to set. I decided to move on, not knowing where I was going.

I was not sure if the smell down here was getting better or I had become immune to it.

16

As I continued walking, I concentrated on my dire situation. "Who is after me? Why are they after me?"

I knew I would be discovered soon. "I have no survival skills. I don't think I am going to make it out here. I was nearly beaten by a drunk human. How can I defend myself against the Enthol? Why did I run? I will never get away." I was ready to give up when I felt the moonlight through a broken utility hole cover. I felt its call. It was so strong, so intense that I had to go to it. But there was no ladder up to the utility hole cover above.

"If I die tonight, I will have died knowing the call of the moon in the human world. I would have lived as a true vampire." I balled my fist, demanding my tears not to fall.

"I am a vampire, a true prince of the night. I can do anything; I have the power." And then I jumped with all my ability. I went higher and higher. I hit my head on the utility hole cover as I barreled through to the top. I hit the ground hard, about five feet from the opening. Luckily no one saw my blunder.

I took a deep breath, finally getting to smell the fresh air of the human world. The atmosphere was like the atmosphere of the vampire world. One of the differences was the freshness of the sky. The vampire wars destroyed most of our trees and vegetation, causing our air to smell stale.

I looked around this foreign land in amazement. So much of this place seemed familiar, but it was also very different. The trees here were lush and green. I stared at them, aided by the moonlight. The buildings here were similar to the architecture of the vampire world. The significant difference was the windows; they did not have sun dampeners that came down to block the sun's rays.

In the distance, I noticed a clothing store. The vampire world kept tabs on the human world and events that might affect our world, although we had sworn not to interfere. We learned of the trends and fashion of the humans. As a Keeper, I hoped to one day visit the human world to collect data and maybe find a link between humans and vampires.

Male and female clothing etiquette was one of the similarities our worlds shared. We vampires had a combined fashion that was reminiscent of the Renaissance era. We still wore tunics, surcoats, and tabards, but our pants were more like modern American denim pants. Another difference was that the material we used to make our clothing felt more like a soft velvet from head to toe.

I had viewed these human shows in passing, never giving them my full attention. I did pick up on the differences between the outfits human males and females wore.

18

"If it's a male store, then I'm in luck," I mumbled to myself as I rubbed the lump on my head.

I saw a sign on the top of the building. The sign read "Flea Market." I had heard of these stores; they were not the top tier of human fashion outlet stores.

"A flea market—oh well, beggars can't be choosers. Now how do I get in?"

I made my way to the back of the building and saw a door with bars on it. I pulled at it with my dominant hand; it budged, barely. I worked my other arm into the bars and gave it another try. The door pulled away from the hinges, and I stumbled back clumsily. I shook the door off my arm. The clang of the metal hitting the concrete echoed in the silent night. I squatted down and froze, hoping no one was around to hear.

"The coast is clear," I said to myself as I walked into the building. After about fifteen minutes of walking around corners, I finally found the door to the main store.

I laughed to myself. "I wonder if I am the first vampire ever to get lost."

I carefully inspected the clothes. I did not know much about human fashion as I thought I did. I knew I needed more than just my traditional vampire shrouds if I wanted to blend in. I need to cover my arm not that I was embarrassed by my disability, but the more I blended in with the norm, the easier it will be to walk among them.

I grabbed a pair of pants and the baggiest, droopiest shirt I could find, and a ball cap. I then swapped my bag for a backpack. I dressed and headed out the door. I was proud of myself. After a few minutes, I found my way out of the store and headed down the street.

The more I walked into town, the more people were around. Soon I was in a crowd; people were looking at me with pity in their eyes. I saw a young lady cutting her eyes toward me and whispering to the woman beside her.

There was a group of men huddled around a car. One of the men pointed and tapped another man on the shoulder and laughed out loud.

I saw a sign that read "Augusta College," and it dawned on me, colleges had libraries.

"I need to get into the Sharuk program, but how? The guy on the phone said we were kindred, and that he was a Keeper like me. I wonder if I can link into the program through a human computer," I mumbled to myself, which drew even more attention to me.

It felt like I had traveled for hours. Finally, I reached the campus library. It was late—almost four in the morning. I saw a sign on the door: "Library hours 8 a.m. to 8 p.m."

"Darn, I will have to come back, too many people around to break in," I whispered under my breath. I gave a tug at the door, and it opened. "Maybe I can sneak in and out without anyone noticing"

When I walked inside, I saw a lady behind the desk, so I approached her. As I neared the counter she looked and jumped.

"Whoa, you startled me. The library is closed!" The young lady spoke as if relieved that she was in no danger.

I was thrown off guard. "I need to log on to your computer and find some information, Lilly," I requested, getting her name from her name tag.

Lilly was about five foot seven. She had curly light brown hair that glistened with gold streaks in the light of the library. Lilly also had burgundy curly locks that intertwined with her normal hair. I could not tell if she was a very tan white girl or if she was of another ethnicity.

"Like I said, we're closed," Lilly replied in a stern voice as if she were talking to a child.

Now I was getting upset. Never in my two hundred and five years had I been spoken to in such a way. I was also getting antsy, as I felt the sun starting to ascend. I tried to rationalize with her so that she could understand my desperation.

"Look you will help me, now!" I demanded.

"Yes, I will help you," Lilly answered in an exhausted tone.

"Wow, I didn't know I could do that," I said to myself. I had heard of vampires putting humans under a trance, but this was my first inter-action with one. Maybe this was how other vampires kept their victims from fighting back.

"First I need a place to rest," I said, realizing that the sun would be up before I would have completed my task.

"My place isn't far from here; come with me," she requested.

"That would be fine. Let's go," I replied.

We got into her automobile. It looked like an old teal green, pregnant roller skate. The inside of the car was tattered with soda cans and paper cylinders. The smell of ash and stale air billowed out of the car as I opened the door. I did not complain because beggars can't be choosers, even though I was in charge—I hoped. We reached her apartment about twenty minutes later. Lilly's apartment was on the second floor of a long, narrow building. I had a feeling that this building was once a hotel of some sort. I wondered if the tenants paid the monthly hotel rate or more.

Down a long corridor toward the end was our destination.

"We are here," Lilly reported as she opened the door.

Her apartment seemed to hand off the ashtray stench like a relay baton.

I felt too drained to let the smell bother me. I had slept in worse-smelling places within the last twenty-four hours. I looked around for a place to rest that would not cause me to burst into flames when the sun rose.

I crawled into the dark hole of her hall closet and rested. I was getting hungry again and needed to feed, but not from her. I could not kill her; she was the closest thing to an ally I had.

Lilly went to sleep in her bedroom. Waking up, she continued her routine as if last night never happened. She attended her classes as usual and returned home to prepare for her job at the library. I heard her come in the door and put down her keys.

"Why is it so dark in here?" Lilly asked, walking toward the curtains to let in the sunlight.

I came out of the closet and stretched. She turned around and screamed. Her reaction surprised me, and I took a step back.

"What the hell? How'd you get in my apartment?" she screamed

"You don't remember me?" I said in a panic.

"Yeah, you are the retarded guy who wanted something in the library!" Lilly blurted, unconcerned about the words coming out of her mouth.

"You need to calm down and sit." My voice was stern and strong; I had never used that tone with anyone before, but I knew I couldn't let this escalate further.

Lilly sat and took a breath, but she was far from calm. "Who are you?"

"My name is Zarian Kane; I am a Keeper," I said, trying to keep things simple.

"You know, whichever hospital you escaped from, they will want you back. They will find you." Her words came out harsh and cruel.

23

"I escaped to the human world. I worked in a library; I do sort of what you do. As a fellow Librarian, I am in need of your help. You said I was in a hospital? I haven't been to any hospital. What gives you that impression."

Lilly took a minute, staring at me from top to bottom. "Well, for starters, just by looking at you anyone can tell you are handicapped. I am not talking about your arm; I am talking about your haircut. You would have fairly decent curly brown hair if it weren't shaped like a dirty Q-tip.

"Even if you weren't physically disabled, we could tell by the way you dress. I mean, who wears a fluorescent orange Hawaiian shirt with neon-green palm trees and that bright yellow ball cap. Whoever dressed you should have been fired for being cruel." Lilly let out a puff of air and smirked while crossing her arms. If she were a cartoon, there would be steam coming from her ears.

"I dressed myself! Green for the base of the tree, orange for the foliage, and yellow representing the sun. Was this not correct?" I pouted; my sense of accomplishment shriveled away slowly, and in the emptiness, self-doubt started to grow.

"Look, the truth is I am a vampire." Before I could finish the sentence, she began to laugh.

"Okay, I get it; this is one of those college pranks. I don't have time for this." Lilly looked around, trying to spot the hidden cameras.

"This is no joke," I said in my newly learned stern voice. This time I showed a little fang for effect. I think I went too far, because she jumped up and tried to break for the door. I jumped up and blocked her in. I held my hands up, palms held high, trying to de-escalate the situation.

24

"Look, I need your help. If I wanted you dead, I would have killed you last night," I said in a deep whisper almost like a reverse yell. I hoped to sound more convincing to her than I did to myself.

"Just have a seat and—"

"No, you look! You can't just come in here, barking orders like you the big boss," she interrupted. Her left arm flailed around, accenting her words, yet her right pointer finger seemed to stay focused on me.

"Okay, Lilly. Can we talk for a minute?" I asked politely. In the back of my mind, I tried to figure why I could not control her mind like last night. If I could put her in a trance, this predicament would be less awkward.

"I just need to get into your library's computer; they will be coming for me soon."

"Who? Vampire hunters?" she asked, only a hint of sarcasm still in her voice.

"You could say that. I am being charged with a crime I did not commit, and unless I can sort this out, I will be killed. So, I will ask you again: Will you please help me?"

"No," Lilly blurted out, then paused. "I don't need to get involved. This is my second year of college, I am working my butt off just to stay above water, and I don't need this drama. I don't want to get involved. Do you know how hard I am struggling just trying to make decent grades? College medical books are not designed to cater to dyslexic students. I work in the library to get the extra time. It takes me longer to read through the information properly," she reiterated.

"I do not know the word dyslexic. I would think that those of us that do not fit in the norm should stick together. In my world, if you do not prove yourself useful, you are put to death," I said to her, grasping at her empathy.

"Dyslexia is a learning disorder. I have a problem connecting words and sounds to their letters. As I read, I don't track words well; sometimes I read the same line twice in a sentence. Counselors told me I shouldn't get into the medical field, but I will prove them wrong. That's why I can't help you. I've got too much going on to get involved with whatever you are caught up in." Lilly sounded exhausted. It was obvious she had given this speech before, or at least a version of it.

25

"I am sorry you feel that way—or I will be," I said under my breath as I turned around and headed out the door. I didn't want to force her; violence seemed so barbaric.

I stepped into the hallway and clung to the wall. The sun was still out. I felt the heat even though the light did not touch me. I winced as I felt the burn down in my soul.

As I moved further into the hall, Lilly grabbed my shoulder and pulled me back inside.

"Sorry, I don't want to get involved, but the least I could do is get you a better outfit to wear."

I looked at her curiously. "I thought that this was how all humans dressed."

"Only if you are in the circus," she replied. "Lucky for you I sleep in men's pullovers."

I followed her toward her bedroom, still wondering what was wrong with my human ensemble.

"First of all, your clothes are too loud. You should dress less distracting if you don't want to be noticed. We are about the same height, so these sweats should fit you comfortably," she said as she reached into her closet and pulled out various items of clothing.

The sweats were all grey with Augusta College across the chest of the shirt and on the legs of the pants. To say that the sleeves were a little long was an understatement. The cuff of the oversized sweatshirt swallowed the palm of my dominant hand.

With embarrassment in her tone, Lilly spoke. "You know, I always imagined vampires were a little taller and umm, well, not umm handicapped. I mean, in the movies they are handsome and perfect; I mean perrrfect," she said, stressing the word with a tone of desire and yearning.

"Vampires are like you humans; we are all shapes and sizes. The few of us that are not PERFECT, as you say, are taken away as children and given certain tasks in our society. We become historians called Keepers, or in some cases locked away as experiments and tortured. It was a tough life for us; we are forbidden to cohabitate with females, even if they are like us. They did not want us to breed more of our kind."

Today was the first time I had ever spoken of our mistreatment to anyone. I found it odd that I had never openly spoken of our injustice. I dreamt that all Keepers would one day be treated as equals. The heat of emotion passed, and I continued.

"We were not even allowed to think of our treatment, lest a stronger vampire reads our thoughts. Speaking against the king's law is considered treason, punishable by death, death by sunlight." My head felt heavy as I spoke; suddenly my vision got blurry. I rubbed my fingers over my eyes and found water on my hands.

"They are called tears," Lilly says. "Haven't you ever cried before?"

"Not in two hundred and five years. Nor have I ever thought to speak my mind or have these feelings. I think that I have been under a spell or trance. What if the entire village is under a trance?"

A lightbulb came on in my head. "The further I got from the village, the more my instincts and strength began to work."

"Where is your village? Why haven't we humans ever seen it?" Lilly asked, like a curious child wondering about the monster at the end of the book.

"Well, it's difficult to explain; before you fall asleep, do you sometimes feel yourself starting to dream? Our world and yours are like that. We are like a mirror world of yours. We are sharing the same sun, moon, and sky, we are on the same time plane and location, but we are on a different plane of existence, which is why vampires can't see their reflection in mirrors. To us, it is like looking out the window." I tried to explain, but somehow confused myself a little.

Another idea came to mind. "Windows! That's how I can access the vampire computer system."

"As if I wasn't confused already—what the heck are ya talkin' 'bout now!" Lilly exclaimed, trying to keep up.

"Have you ever had a sudden computer freeze up on you then crash, leaving just a blank blue screen? Well, that wasn't just a plain blue screen; that was one of us using your computer system through your actual computer line. It is our best way to keep current on what is happening in your world."

"What do you mean, you access our computers? Are you the ones responsible for identity theft? Innocent people's lives are destroyed, or when they have to pay to get computer repairs done." Lilly seemed a little peeved.

"No, no, my friend—we only research. Any tampering of that sort is strictly forbidden. Besides, what would we gain? Nothing from your world matters in ours."

A dark shadow appeared under the front door, followed by a knock. The three rapid but forceful taps were distinctly familiar. I knew who it was.

Lilly spoke out of reflex before I could stop her "Who is it?"

"Ma'am, we need to talk. We believe you are harboring a fugitive. Open up, and you may leave without any consequences," the voice behind the door said.

It was the tan Enthol; I will call him Agent Tan. I guessed he was the senior guy or the spokesman for the two, or worse, maybe the other was more action and less talk. Either way, they were both there, although only one was at the door.

"Don't let them in; they have no power if you don't let them in. That is one of the powered possessions that humans have. The power of threshold—it makes the playing field even." I said in my new shout/whisper voice.

Just then the door came crashing down. "I hear you, Mr. Kane. How soon you forget we have excellent hearing."

"Yes, and bad manners too," I said, swinging my fist at him wildly. He blocked it with ease and front-kicked me in the stomach. Never had I ever been hit like that before. I buckled to the floor, gasping for air. Lilly was there to save the day, bashing him over the head with her portable stereo. He hit the ground, hard.

"Thank you," I said as I started to get up from the floor, feeling a bit nauseous.

Suddenly an impact like a bus crashed into my back; I was forced face first to the ground. It was Agent Muscles, Enthol number two. My stomach was cramping, my back felt broken, and a cut over my right eye was throbbing blood.

28

I felt something come over me. I saw red—not the blood in my eye red, but rage. I had never felt that angry before. I got up and tackled Agent Muscles. The tackle was hard, and it was fast. I couldn't believe it how fast I moved.

Agent Muscles couldn't believe it either. He was down, and he was out.

Agent Tan was conscious and ready to fight. He turned me around and grabbed me by the throat.

"How dare you? You are not fit to touch us—you are barely a vampire!" he shouted in my face.

"Maybe so, but you, my friend, forget two facts! One, you are only half vampire, and you were not invited in, meaning that your vampire powers were left at the door. Two, I am a full vampire, and your blood is all human right now, making you food." I broke his grip with my dominant arm and jabbed my other arm into his chest. My single-digit appendage went in like a dagger and yanked out his heart. I then commenced drinking his heart's blood. I felt myself begin to heal, and I started to feel better. I wish I could say that Lilly did too, but she was either in shock or unconscious. She was standing there with her eyes wide open, staring at nothing. I had thought that she was under a trance.

I stood up and washed the blood from my face in the kitchen sink. When I turned back around, Agent Muscles was gone.

I walked over to Lilly hoping I could snap her out of the spell. As I approached her, she seemed to come back around on her own.

"Oh, my God! Oh, my God! Oh, my God! What just happened? What did you do? I can't get involved in this; I have to call the police. I can't go to jail; this is your fault! I said I didn't want to get involved," she babbled.

Lilly was shaking her hands as if they were wet—something very girly and not quite what I expected from her. But really, who knows how they would react when put in such a trying situation.

"Calm yourself, girl," I commanded, and she did. I knew then I was weak from hunger earlier and my power over her had withered away. Although I wanted to calm her, I did not wish to control her, because if I lost control at the wrong time—again, it could be deadly for both of us.

"Well, Z, how we gonna get rid of the body, huh? I am not gonna to put him in my fridge, and I am not going to watch you eat him!" Her sarcasm had a sense of urgency and fear. She was with me but not controlled by me.

Funny thing about half-hybrid vampires; they carry some of the same traits as full vampires. You see, a full vampire cannot enter a human domicile without permission, but half-hybrids can. When a half-hybrid enters a human domicile without permission, they essentially leave the vampire side at the door. "I have a theory," I said.

Grabbing Agent Tan's pants leg, I tossed him out the front door opening. His head bounced off the side of the door frame. He burst into flames and was reduced to ash in a matter of seconds.

"When he broke in, I guess he forgot he became human; his entire body was human. Because he was not invited in, all vampire traits and powers were left at the door. When I tossed him out of your domicile—uh, your home—his vampire essence reconnected to his body. His dead human body, connected to the vampire essence in the sunlight, equals ash. I assumed that the vampire trait was dominant, or he wouldn't be an Enthol."

"What! You threw a dead body into my hallway because you assumed it would turn to ash! And what is an Enthol, again?" Lilly was a getting revved up again.

"Enforcers of the law, for your safety. That's all you need to know about them."

"Wait, if they enforce the law, then you are a criminal." She had her left hand on her hip, and the right finger was pointing at me again.

"Just like a white girl; soon as you see a black man in sweats and a hoodie you assume he is a thug." I tried to imitate a rapper from an old *Yo MTV Raps* episode. As I heard myself say it, I knew I had failed in the attempt.

"Uhm, no you didn't! First of all, I am half black— don't let the blond curls fool you!" She rotated her head, and for an instant, it looked as if it were going to fall off.

Focused back on the topic, and much calmer, she continued. "It's simple math; cops are after you, plus you killed a cop, equals criminal."

"W e need to get out of here before they come back. It's almost seven o'clock. The library will be closing soon," I said, focusing on my agenda.

"Hey, I ain't going with you! I said I wasn't getting involved." She shook her head and stepped away from me.

I did not have time for this, but I did not want to trance her, either. How could I make her do what I wanted? Humans were such finicky creatures.

"Please, I can't do this without you. I know that you don't owe me anything. I forced my way into your life, and I am truly sorry. I am two hundred and five years old and today is the first day that I have been alive—free. I know that I can never repay you for what you have done so far, and I shouldn't ask you for more, but please, please—" I begged.

She raised her hand in mid please and sighed. "I can tell you have a lot of pride and to beg for my help is hard for you. I will take you to the library, but that is as far as I am willing to go with you.

"But first, unless the blood stains on your shirt are going to turn to ash also, you had better change." She handed me another sweatshirt hoodie, the same color with a different logo.

I looked at her with a raised eyebrow. "How many of these do you own?"

"What? They are comfy!" she smirked.

After clumsily pulling on the sweatshirt, I realized that my left non-dominant arm nestled quite nicely in the front pocket and smiled. Lilly rolled her eyes.

I pulled the hood of the sweatshirt over my head. The sun was starting to set. The night sky was becoming cool and inviting, but the sun was not completely gone yet. I felt the trickle of warmth as we trotted off to her car like an old *Batman and Robin* episode.

In the parking lot, the scene of the TV show changed from sitcom to horror. I felt my smile fading; darkness came over me as I realized I was home, back in the village. What kind of magic—no power? Magic revolved around misdirection, planned tricks; this was power, pure and raw. This power took my will to be in the human world. I still didn't know how I got to the human world, and now someone or something has brought me back to the vampire world.

"How did I get here?" I trembled under my voice. It took me a second to realize exactly where I was. I was at the front door of the Enthol's headquarters. "I definitely don't want to be here."

I did what any vampire, human, or any other being would do when faced with danger; I ran for my life. I ducked behind garbage cans and automobiles, trying to stay hidden. I was an easy target to spot in these human clothes. I knew if I went home, the Enthol would be waiting.

"Professor Jeremiah—he will help me, he must!" I said as I crept through the back road and alleyway through the night. Finally, I reached the professor's domicile.

Moments after my birth, I was dropped off at the library that would be my home for the next 195 years. Over this time, I had learned a lot about the professor. I learned that the professor did not smoke, though he always had his old briar pipe with him. He said it made him feel more distinguished.

When the professor walked down the halls of the library, he always walked slowly. His right foot was about six inches shorter than his left foot. His left foot twisted outward at an odd angle, causing him to need crutches. His poor mobility was not the reason he slowly walked the halls. He paced slowly because he said he could feel the power of knowledge coursing through the walls.

Professor Jeremiah was not just his title; it was his lifestyle. His salt-and-pepper hair was always tousled and messy. He wore various earth-toned doublets—a jacket similar to the jackets worn in the Renaissance era around the 14th century. The brown and tan colors gave his pale white skin a warmer, more lively hue.

I made my way to the back window of the professor's domicile. I peered into his window and saw him with his trademark unlit pipe in his mouth. He was enjoying a glass of blood and reading a huge book.

I tapped on the window to get the attention of my mentor, the only father figure I have ever known.

"Professor, Professor—it is I, Zarian."

"Go away. You have brought disgrace upon yourself, to our profession, and now you try to bring disgrace to my home." There was sadness in his voice. "I thought of you as a son; we were all taken from our homes as children, and our work made us a family."

"Please, Professor, let me in," I pleaded.

"There is no bond stronger than family; family is what gives us a kindred strength." The professor took a breath, "You have betrayed your family; you have disrupted our home."

"No, Professor, I have not. I was framed! I would never betray-"

33

A noise, a voice in my head stopped me mid-sentence.
"Run, child, run!" I don't know why, but I did. Down one alley-way and across to another alley, I ran as fast as my legs could carry me.

Then there was a flash of dark, and—I was back in the human world. I could see the flea market where I had gotten my first human clothes. I felt the cold night air and knew in an instant that only an hour or so had passed. I was sure the library was closed. A simple mission such as getting to the library was becoming a journey.

"What has happened to my little friend?" I murmured to myself.

I spun around 360 degrees and tried to get my bearings. I searched my mind trying to find how to get to the library. Like a virtual reality map or a replay in HD, I saw the last two days flash before me.

I sniffed the cold night air trying to get a sense of the path I took, and trying to get to the library.

In my human clothing, I walked in the open. This time as I walked down the sidewalk, I was not getting as many glares from the people at the college campus as I neared the entrance. I believed the college name and logo on my clothing played a part in that, not vampire ability.

In the distance, I saw the stairs to the building that led to the li-brary. As I drew closer to the stairs, I saw a girl sitting on the stairs, and I instantly knew who it was.

Lilly was sitting there. She seemed a bit out of sorts. Could be because of the day we'd both had. I was sure under other circumstances she was a delightful human to have a conversation with about the similarities and differences of our worlds. Now was not one of those circumstances. I took a deep breath as I approached her. She looked up with tears in her eyes.

"You shouldn't have come! I told you that I didn't want to get involved." She pressed her lips together.

At that moment, I knew it was a trap. I looked back and saw two Enthols walking toward me. I could tell they were Enthols because of the outfits they all chose to wear. Although the Enthol have traditional uniforms in the vampire world, they dressed differently in the human world.

The Enthols chose to wear black tactical-style pants, black leather hiking boots, and a black shirt, hidden behind a black hooded trench coat. To close out the less- than-stealthy outfits, they wore a pair of obnoxious sunglasses, even at night. The sunglasses were a cross between Ray-Bans and swim goggles. The Enthol wore these sunglasses to prevent humans from seeing their vampire eyes. They also wore them to stop vampires from knowing which of the Enthols had human eyes.

The two Enthols were tall, lean, and pale. They could have been full vampires, but I could not tell. Since they looked like total vampires, I was sure they were very powerful. I was in trouble—more trouble, if that were possible.

"I'm sorry," she whispered, daring not to look me in the eyes. She had her arms wrapped in a way that seemed like she was holding herself. I could tell she was remorseful for being the bait in the trap.

I touched her shoulder and looked forward. Four more Enthols were coming toward me. I felt like a trapped human.

I hadn't fed enough to take them on—one maybe, but six? No way! I chuckled to myself as I thought of how a homeless drunk and two Enthols in human form almost bested me.

I could not outrun them. My limp, although very faint and barely noticeable, prevented me from making a proper running stride—although I was quicker than any human. Physically I was no match for these guys.

I shook my head and looked down at Lilly. A vampire grimace came across my face, both fanged and fearsome. "I may not be physically equal to them, but they are not mentally equal to me."

I took my arm out of the pocket of my hoodie and hunched my back a little more than usual. I tried to make myself look more vulnerable to the crowd. I began to yell. "Puppy has anybody theen my bown puppy?" I walked toward the nearest human begging for help. I felt sick to my stomach portraying myself is such a demeaning manner, but the alternative was worse. I knew that if I did not get Lilly and myself to safety, we would not survive the night.

"Could u help me find my bown puppy?" I continued, playing on the sympathy of the humans in the area.

A white college student, female, blonde hair, blue eyes walked toward me. "Aww, so sorry, which way did he go?"

"Not he!" I shouted. "Puppy dog girl, dog – arf, arf" I rubbed my lips as if wiping off the spit.

She began to shout out to other people near us including the Enthol. "This guy lost his puppy, could you help us find it?" She smiled at me. *What a good Samaritan*, I thought!

This course of events surprised the Enthols. They looked at each other, not knowing what to do. They had the power and the numbers to rush us and take us away, but the cost of being discovered was too high. The Enthol knew that one camera phone at the right angle at the right time could reveal more than the human world was ready to know.

Lilly got up and joined the make-believe search. "It'd be a lot faster if you and your frat boys helped out!" she shouted, looking over to the nearest Enthol approaching from the rear.

The Enthol walked past her, not willing to play our game. They were beside me now.

"Come quietly, Mr. Kane! This charade is over!" one of the tall, slender Enthols whispered in my ear, grabbing me by the arm. His hair was straight, shoulder length, and black as tar. Under the moonlight, his smooth, pale white skin had a green undertone. The Enthol beside him was a copycat; the only exception was that his black hair was closely cropped on the sides

"I yelled out; you did it! You did it! You took my puppy!" I jerked away from him.

My blonde Samaritan came to my aid. "Get away from him, creep! What do you think you are doing?"

He looked down at her and was about to possess her when I stepped in front of him to break his eye contact.

"You took my puppy away!" I shouted at him.

He grabbed for my arm again. This time I jerked away and fell on the floor. More people had gathered to view the drama unfolding in front of the library.

The blonde tried to push my bully away from me, but he didn't budge; his clothing barely gave way to the pressing of her tiny hands. Her heroism faded as the basic instinct of fear began.

She yelled out, "Someone help me get this jerk away from here."

I don't know how or where they came from, but a mob of humans suddenly appeared around us.

Lilly chimed in as if on cue, "Yeah, and take your friends with you."

Suddenly attention was drawn across to the other four Enthols. The mob began to circle, closing in on the six tall predators as if they were the prey. If only the humans knew how much danger they were in, they would run in horror.

I knew the first laws of all vampires was to hide our existence from humans . . . and so did they. The Enthols was established for this very reason, among other things.

36

When the blonde turned her head toward the mob and away from me, I ran—fast.

I was around the corner and up the street in a flash, or close enough.

I got away this time, but they would be coming for me. I heard the honk of a horn and looked down the street. It was Lilly's car.

I ran toward it and fumbled off the curb, stumbling toward her car. I came to an abrupt stop as my forehead hit her driver's side front tire. As I staggered across the front and flailed into the seat, she drove off.

"I guess the grace and charm of vampires is a myth too," she mumbled as she looked out the rearview to see—well, I don't know what she was trying to see, since vampires have no reflection.

"I was thinking about what you said about needing a computer," Lilly said softly.

I could tell by the strain in her voice that she was not accustomed to talking so low.

I whispered back to her, "Why are you talking so?" As I looked over to her, she wasn't there anymore.

I was back, back in front of the Enthol headquarters. This time around, I must have lost time, because dawn was quickly approaching.

I raced back down the alley behind the dumpster and saw the utility hole cover I first entered at the beginning of my quest.

"Hello, old friend," I said, pulling up the lid and climbing down the familiar dark hole. I proceeded down the tunnel and found a corner to rest. I tried to look around and could not tell if this was the same path I took before. I found a spot I was fairly sure the sunlight would not reach. I huddled in a fetal position and was out like a light.

A red flash of light blanked my mind, and I could not wake up. I was in a trance while I slept. I knew that whatever powerful force had me, meant me no harm. I rode the trance like a rip current, flowing with it until the opportunity arose for me to break free and run. The purpose of the trance was a link between this invader and myself. The invader was careful not to show too much of themselves to me, but I could gather that the visions were through the eyes of a female.

The vampire war was long and bloody. The land, the ocean, the vampires, and all creatures were nearly annihilated. Through the chaos, two kingdoms still stood tall. A treaty was drawn, and the lands were divided between the nations of the Drak and the Vlad.

The Drak were skilled tacticians, thinkers, and planners. King Ravvi, referred to as Ravvi the Drak, was elected by a council to be their king and has had total rule over the land and its people since 1637, fifteen years into the war. It is 2017 now, and Ravvi has been the longest-reigning king in Drak history.

One of the strange things about vampires is our aging process. Vampires seemed to have frozen in time at a certain age; then they began to age slowly after a few hundred years. The Drak typically age like humans until they are about twenty years old. Then, they seem only to age a day after every ten years. The effect is they look as if they are in their twenties even though they are potentially a century old.

Ravvi the Drak looked as if he were in his mid-thirties, yet he was over three thousand years old. His sandy brown hair looked like a crown of beautiful feathers on his head and fell to his shoulders. He had high cheekbones and a piercing glare which made him look like he was always pondering something.

Ravvi the Drak often wore royal blue, the royal color of the Drak. Royal-blue shirts seemed to make the pale skin of the Drak glow with a blue tint. Drak were usually between six feet to six feet four inches tall.

The Drak believed that the king should remain in power until he was no longer worthy of the title. When the king was no longer fit to rule, there was a vote to replace him. If the current king refused to relinquish the crown, he and his family were forcefully removed. Since the beginning of time, no king had ever gone against the vote of the council.

Ravvi the Drak was a ruthless strategist, who would rather pollute the land for a thousand years than surrender it to an enemy—burning down an entire forest to find rebel hideouts, dredging giant fire moats for a strategic advantage. The Drak created a burning mist to destroy their enemy from the inside out. The Drak were a danger to all who opposed them in the world of the vampire. Throughout history, there were other vampire colonies and kingdoms who tried to stand up to the Drak and failed. All had failed, except the Vlad clan.

38

The Vlad clan were warriors from birth. Their entire culture revolved around the art of battle. To lead the Vlad, a warrior had
to complete three trials called the Trials of Leadership. The trial of
the mind was designed to test intelligence, the trial of the soul was
designed to test inner strength, and the trial of the body pitted you
against the other competitors to ensure the strongest will be the leader.

The warrior to win the trials of leadership earned the title Vlad
de Czar. For the past 600 years, the reigning Vlad de Czar was Joshua
Ericks.

The Vlad were one of the few species of vampires that had a small
muscle tone. The Vlad were tall and intimidating. Their skin color
ranged from tan to deep dark ebony, with a bronze undertone.

The war between the Drak and the Vlad was devastating. The two
kingdoms nearly destroyed the planet until the visual of an actual river
of blood caused the battling kingdoms and the smaller colonies to call
a truce.

The vampire world was divided and the smaller colonies, which
totaled six, had to choose which kingdom to serve, or perish.

The Congregation Council was established to keep the peace and
civility between the kingdoms. The Congregation Council was com-
prised of three pure species of vampires from the Drak, three pure

species of vampires from the Vlad, and one pure species vampire from the six remaining colonies. The requirement of pure blood ensured that mind control of the members would not happen. The Enthol was designed to enforce the rules of the Congregation Council; this would help the balance of power remain neutral. Neither kingdom would step in and force their control or dominance.

The red glow of the trance continued to wash over me, as I lost all sense of time. I was mentally somewhere in the past, while I was physically in the present. As I continued to follow the trance on my journey, I learned more about the vampire wars than any library could ever teach.

Long ago there were so many different types of vampires that it was impossible to classify them all. Over the last few centuries, the war had destroyed entire species of vampires—each species of vampire shares similar qualities and traits like telepathy, and heightened vision and hearing.

Some species had qualities that were unique to their species like shapeshifting, flying, and the ability to walk in the day. When the war began, the day walkers were the first to be destroyed. The next to fall was the shapeshifters, followed by the flyers. As of now, there are only eight species left.

A group of vampires from different cultures got together to help preserve their way of life before the war wiped them out of exitance. These vampires were the first genealogists and historiographers of the historical documents which would become the Sharuk. The preservation of the vampire history was important enough for both kingdoms to give sanctuary to all Keepers. There were various libraries in both kingdoms and a master library outside of the kingdoms. The Congregation Council ensured that the master library stayed neutral.

As the landscape and culture started to change, so did the vampires. Some vampires became intolerant of other vampire cultures, in their fight for self-preservation.

Some vampires crossed cultural lines and mated out of their species, but the offspring had the traits of either the mother or the father, not both. There were cases of vampires who went to the human world and had children with humans. These half-species possessed partial traits of a vampire, like speed, heightened vision, or enhanced hearing. These traits were vastly superior to humans but could not compare to those of a pure vampire.

The Congregation Council were the first to see the potential use for a being that could handle vampire affairs in the daylight. The Congregation Council established a task force to protect and serve the vampire civilization. This task force was called the Enforcers of the Law—Enthol for short.

The Enthols were a combination of all remaining vampire species. The half-species were mostly field operators. Field operators could go into the daylight and perform vampire duties in the human world if a vampire found themselves trapped in the human world, either by incarceration or other factors that would cause them to be caught in the daylight. The Enthol would act to keep the vampire's existence a secret.

I could tell that this part of the trance was significant. When I tried to inquire why, my focus shifted to the window.

It was almost dawn. The screams of a woman in pain echoed through the chambers of the Vlad de Czar's castle. The queen was in the trials of childbirth.

"You would think that a child of the night would wait until night to be born," King Ravvi the Drak smirked as he stroked his queen's hair. "Is there anything more I can do for you, my lover?"

"Yes, my king," Queen Chanti sneered up to him. "If it isn't too much of a bother, could you get this child out of me!" she screamed

"We are nearly there, your highness." The doctor tried to comfort the royal family. With one last push, there was silence and then a baby's wail.

"It's a boy!" the doctor exclaimed

The nurse gasped in fear. "I don't understand; how could this be?"

Those were the last words the nurse ever spoke. In a flash, the nurse's throat was gushing blood. The doctor also collapsed to the floor in a bloody heap.

The queen squeezed her eyes shut as blood sprayed in her face.

Ravvi the Drak yelled, "Guards, we are under attack." Then he leaped out the window into the daylight. Smoke billowed from his body as he ran down the alleyway and around a corner.

The royal guards rushed into the room to find the doctor and nurse dead on the floor. The queen, exhausted and in tears, still lay on the bed.

"Your highness, what has happened? Where is the king?" one of the guards asked in a panic.

"The window," she said, wearily pointing at the open window. "He . . . then went out the window. My baby is gone?" The statement came out of her mouth as a question.

Moments later, the king returned; his clothes are charred, his skin was burned, and his energy was low. Worst of all, he was holding a baby; the child was dead. Upon seeing this, the royal guards knelt and looked away.

41

"What has happened your highness, my king?" Melville, the head guardsman, asked.

"One vampire—he was fast, even in the daylight. He could not have been half; he must have been wearing some sort of protection. I was almost upon him when—" Ravvi the Drak looked down at his son; tears fell to the broken child's body. "Someone will pay for this!" His eyes turned crimson red, and his wounds healed immediately; the royal guard gasped as the room filled with power pouring from the king.

"Leave us," the queen said as she reached for the child.

"How did the child not heal itself as Ravvi the Drak did?" Sal, the royal guard's second-in-command, asked suspiciously.

"Some powers are dormant at birth; some are there, but the use of their power has to be learned. Regardless, these matters are not our concern. Our concern is to find how an intruder got into the kingdom undetected and how they got away," Melville responded.

"Inform the Gray Guards we need to find a trail or some lead; we need to find the traitor before Ravvi the Drak turns his rage to us."

"Yes, sir." Sal saluted. "Did you feel his power? It felt like I was drowning in hot air. That was him at his weakest? In daylight? I now see why he is King of the Drak. His power is unfathomable!"

"Indeed, his is a direct descendant of the Ancient Ones! Get to your task, and report back to me before you go to rest," Melville ordered.

S al instructed the Gray Guard of their tasks, then took the underground chambers to his home.

Blake was the chief in charge of the Gray Guard. The Gray Guard
were a group of half-species vampires that oversaw guarding and safe-
keeping the kingdom of the Drak. Unlike the Enthol, their job was not
for the wellbeing of all vampires. The Gray Guards' sole responsibility
was the Drak and any affairs Ravvi the Drak deemed Drak business.

It had only been a few hundred years since half-species became
an acceptable term. When it was daytime, and a vampire's domicile
caught fire, they were grateful for a half-species to rescue them and
hopefully save their home. If trapped in the human world and daylight
was coming, vampires were happy to see the half-species.

A strange phenomenon occurred in the vampire genetics. Two
species of vampires could have children, and those children would
have traits of only one of the parents. A half-species could have char-
acteristics of both parents, which was why they were able to go out
into the day, and still have vampire abilities. On some rare occasions,
a half-species would mate with a different species of vampire, and that
child could have the traits of both parents and grandparents.

To date, there had not been a case of two half-species with double
traits mating; that powerful offspring would be scary interesting.

The term half-species started as a negative term, but instead of fighting for their respect, they kept it, owned it, and made it a positive term. Some even changed their name to "Half-species" to make sure the vampire they saved called them Mister or Miss Half-species. Some vampires still negatively referred to the term half-species.

Vampires usually turned their noses up when walking past a half-species. Half-species were avoided and shunned until they were needed; then, of course, the vampires were grateful the half-species were there to help.

43

The half-species had become an essential part of vampire society. The half-species were woven so deep that vampires could no longer exist without them. The half-species were sent out into the kingdom looking for the traitor that murdered the son of Ravvi the Drak.

For all half-species in the kingdom, this was a personal mission. It was Ravvi the Drak who saw the potential of half-species well before he became king of the Drak. Even though it took a few thousand years, the Drak was the first to classify half-species as citizens. Once he became king, Ravvi the Drak created the Gray Guard and handpicked the half-species to be trained.

Blake was one of the first half-species to be recruited. Blake worked his way up the ranks and earned his spot on the Gray Guard. Some speculated that he could be the captain of the royal guard if he desired. Blake had declined the proposal to be nominated several times in the past two hundred years or more that he had been on the Gray Guard. Blake owed so much to Ravvi the Drak, both personally and for his fellow half-species. Finding the traitor was more than just a priority for him.

44

Sal had returned to his domicile and was about to turn in for the day. But first, he muttered to himself, "Your Highness, I have news that is of utmost importance." A telepathic link was established, and a ghostly form of Sal appeared in the royal chambers.

"It is almost daylight; this better be good, Sally!" a voice murmured.

"Oh, it is, sire. And I wish you wouldn't call me that."

"Come now; as a king I rarely get to revisit my youthful pleasures. Picking on you as a child was one of my best childhood memories. Besides, I will call you what I please, but if anyone else does, I will rip their head off!"

"Yes, sire, as you wish." Sal continued, "The important news is that the king's son has been murdered."

"No, you don't say! Who, pray tell, do they think is the killer of babies?" inquired Joshua Ericks, the king of the Vlad clan, also known as Vlad de Czar.

"I know what you are thinking, brother, but no—Ravvi the Drak has not said it was your doing, yet. Was this your doing brother?" Sal asked.

"No, it was not. I am the slayer of warriors, not children. Stay involved but stay safe. Keep me informed of any interesting developments."

"I will, my czar, my true king," Sal said and broke the link.

As bright day sky faded into nightfall, the kingdom of the Vlad woke up. The czar's court and council were scurrying around more busily than usual. The last of the sunlight had barely left the sky when the news of Ravvi the Drak's son spread throughout the land.

The news of the death reached the kingdom early that night, although the czar knew of the event already. He wanted to wait to see when his court would get the news to him.

This was his way of seeing how fast information got to him and how accurate it was. It was always a tricky situation. If the data was wrong and he knew, the question of how he knew would arise. The last thing he wanted to do was give up his source and betray his brother.

The Czar de Vlad had a few options to consider. He could rally his army and prepare for war and be the first to break the peace treaty. The treaty stated that neither kingdom would show any sign of force to intimidate or incite the other kingdom.

He could wait for Ravvi the Drak to wage war. Not attacking first would leave him vulnerable in the initial attack. An attack could cause his people to suffer, and he would most definitely lose his crown. A warrior king not prepared for war would be shameful.

No, this is not an option, Vlad de Czar thought. *I have the perfect political plan that will put me in a great tactical position.*

As if on cue, Tiel Boax, Chieftain of the Czar Guard, knocked on the chamber door.

The Czar Guard were the warriors picked by the czar to maintain order in the kingdom and ensured the bidding of the king was followed. It was important to note that both kingdoms' security detail made it their duty to keep the Enthol out of the king's affairs.

46

"Vlad de Czar, sorry to bother you, sir. There has been an incident at the Drak kingdom." Chieftain Tiel spoke through the door of the Czar's chamber; using his vampire hearing, he knew the czar was awake.

"Come in, Tiel; give me your report." Vlad de Czar yawned.

"Sir, the Drak kingdom has been attacked. Ravvi, the Drak's child, has been murdered. It will not be long until the suspicions turn toward our kingdom. Shall we prepare for war, my czar?"

"Maybe. Get me a representative of the Congregation Council here immediately. I want all commanders rallied and in the main chamber within the hour. Muster the Czar Guard and put them on alert," Vlad de Czar ordered

"Yes sir, but should we prepare for war?" Chieftain Tiel asked

"You will do what the Vlad de Czar requests with no hesitation! Now leave me."

With that, Chieftain Tiel did an about-face and headed for the door.

"Stop, Tiel; I know that you mean well. I don't mean to be short with you. You are my most dedicated warrior. I know that you are here nearly twenty-four hours a day. You look out for the Vlad kingdom as well as the czar's wellbeing. I have heard of the sacrifices you have gladly made for me and the Vlad kingdom. Right now, I need your faith as well as your dedication." Vlad de Czar gave Chieftain Tiel a small head nod of respect and walked over to his dresser.

Chieftain Tiel turned toward the door again; this time his about-face was a little crisper. Vlad de Czar heard the difference, and he knew at that moment that this man would walk into the daylight wearing gasoline clothes if his czar requested it.

As the sun settled down for its nap, the commanders of the Vlad warrior troops assembled in the courtyard. A gong sounded and the Vlad de Czar made a grand entrance.

The czar was usually in casual attire, but today he wore combat gear—mostly. The czar wore black tactical pants with spiked boots and shin guards. Continuing his ensemble, he had a sword and dagger on his belt.

His shirt was not tactical by any means; it was an aqua blue, button-down, silk embroidered tunic. He was wearing fingerless leather, gauntlet-style gloves, studded with spikes, and a velcro leather wrist support. He wore a crew cut hairstyle, flat top with dreadlocked bangs in the front. His goatee was neatly trimmed and formed a point about two inches below his chin; this effect gave him an elongated face with a sharp masculine jawline.

48

We watched as the Vlad de Czar spoke to his people. I felt the anxiety build and wash over me. I thought my captor wanted me to focus on the speech, so I did.

"Gentlemen, if you would accompany me in the ready room, we have much to discuss." Vlad de Czar gestured for the waiting group to enter a side room.

"Thank you for your prompt response to my request esteemed members of the Congregation Council and my faithful commanders. Word has circulated of the tragedy that has befallen the Kingdom of the Drak. I have thought long of my role as czar and how this news would affect the Vlad. As the czar, it is my job to look out for the well-being of this kingdom. In doing so, I have dressed the part. I am offering my hand in peace but am prepared for war. Council, I want you to relay a message to Ravvi the Drak. Inform him that neither I nor any of my clan had anything to do with this cowardly attack. I am prepared to offer any assistance he requires to ensure justice is served." Vlad de Czar took a breath.

He then looked to his commanders who were sitting in various spots throughout the room. *Is this a coincidence, or are they strategically placed to optimize situation awareness?* he wondered.

"To my commanders, I believe that this attack was intended to make the Vlad look guilty. Although I do not believe Ravvi the Drak will lash out against us, I believe whoever is responsible will make another attempt, maybe toward the Vlad this time. I want the guards doubled around the kingdom."

"Sire, if you rally your army, wouldn't Ravvi the Drak think you are preparing for war?" the Congregation Council member asked.

"I said nothing about rallying an army. I requested the guards be doubled around the kingdom. I do not HAVE an army. I merely have the Czar Guard to protect the kingdom." Vlad de Czar dismissed the council member.

Another Congregation Council member spoke up. "What do you mean you do not HAVE an army? It is true that the Congregation Council handles disputes between the kingdoms, but rogues and marauders are not our affair. Who defends your kingdom, then?

"I never said we are defenseless; we don't need an army. We are ALL warriors!" Vlad de Czar spoke up enthusiastically.

"Hoorah!" one of the commanders shouted.

"We don't have to be wary of our enemies—they need to be wary of US!" Vlad de Czar shouted.

With that, the rest of the commanders started shouting and cheering.

Vlad de Czar waited for the cheers to die down, then sneered at the council members. "Now run along, Congregation Council. Deliver my message; make sure Ravvi the Drak hears every word. I will wait for your response with hope in my heart and a sword in my hand," Vlad de Czar said, then dismissed the group.

49

[Flash of bright red]

The Queen of the Drak was born Marsha Ro-am. She was curled in the corner of the floor of her bedroom, suffocating in the pain and sorrow of her loss. Her official title was Lie't 'at Ravvi le Drak, loosely translated to "bound to Ravvi the Drak."

She and the king were bound together, and Ravvi was bound to the Drak. Ravvi the Drak met his bride-to-be a little over one thousand years ago, while he was surveilling the rebuilding of his war-torn kingdom.

Walking down the side of a canyon wall, he spied a maiden pulling along a fat sow. Some vampires who cannot afford human blood raise pigs and cows to leech their blood and feed their family. Up the trail from her were three men who looked like they were up to mischief.

Ravvi the Drak figured he would leap down to the canyon floor and rush to her aid if necessary. He perched himself on a rock and watched the events as they started to unfold.

Soon the three men were upon the maiden. One grabbed her arm, another grabbed the sow from her other arm, and the third seemed content laughing in her face.

In a flash, the laughing man's throat started spraying blood. No one was holding her arms anymore. The second man arched backward; his heart was ripped from his chest. The third man, the one holding the sow, was chest forward, but his head was turned around backward.

It happened so fast that by the time Ravvi the Drak tensed to jump, the ordeal was over. Ravvi replayed the action in his mind. He could see that the maiden had time to whisper something in the ear of each man before they died. Whatever she said was so horrifying to the men that they died with their eyes wide open, an expression of fear frozen on their faces.

Instantly, Ravvi the Drak knew who she was. He had heard rumors of The Death Whisperer—a woman with a short temper who was so fast and vicious that those who knew of her steered clear of her, and those who had not heard of her soon learned. The only mystery was what she whispered to the victim before their demise—whatever it was, the reaction was always the same.

She had never been punished for murder, because there was never, ever an instance when she instigated the fight.

In most cases, she tried to warn the poor soul, but they never listened, partly because of her milky pale skin and the ever-present silk shawl that flowed around every curve of her full figure. When she spoke, it was as if the moonlight was seducing its lover.

The poise and grace she held before, during, and after the altercation with the three would-be attackers was like a fishing hook in Ravvi the Drak's heart. His days of being a single vampire were numbered.

[Flash of bright red]

Ravvi the Drak pursued Marsha Ro-am cautiously for years. It took over 100 years for her to agree to the marriage. It took Ravvi the Drak the entire courtship to convince her that she would be treated as his equal in every instance.

There was something to be said about a courtship that lasts over a century. The Drak queen and her king were united in mind, body, and soul.

Ravvi the Drak looked down on the floor where his queen lay shivering and sobbing. He knew the dark place his queen was in, he sensed it, and he could feel the emptiness pulling him in with her. Ravvi the Drak knelt on the floor and crawled to her.

"My beloved," he sighed, putting his arms around her. Together they sat on the floor and cried. "One day the gods will find us worthy!" he exhaled.

Upon hearing his words, Marsha stiffened up. "This was you, not the gods!"

51

With a gasp, I woke in the tunnel. It was dark outside. I felt like I was starving.

How long had I been asleep? My arm was throbbing—not hurting, but more like pulsing. I looked at the way my hand formed into its single digit. It was different now; it was shaped more like a talon than a finger. My body felt stronger and tougher, like I had been working out. Yet, I was starving. If I fed, I thought I could take on the world; but there was nothing down here in the sewer.

I climbed the ladder to the top of the sewer; as I neared the opening, I sensed faint wisp of sunlight. That was when I realized the utility hole cover had no holes. The only utility hole covers like that were in my world.

I am back! Again! I said in an exhale. I managed the ladder less awkwardly this time. My grip was stronger, and as I climbed, I didn't lose my breath as fast. I slowly peered through the opening. It was dusk; the last of the sunlight had faded behind the horizon. I gazed around the surroundings, and to my surprise, I was not at the Enthol Headquarters.

In the distance, I saw a library. It was not my library. This one was huge—the biggest library I had ever seen. "The master library. I could find a computer there. I doubt the Enthol would have thought to look for me here," I murmured as I crawled out of the sewer.

Maybe I should peek through the window first. "See, I am learning from my past mistakes," I mumbled to myself.

Inside was a vampire with a curly salt-and-pepper afro, closely cropped on the side that formed an almost mullet silhouette. His thick mustache bristled over his top lip and fluffed down the sides, just below his bottom lip. He had a dark skin tone, but not brown or tan. His skin tone was like coffee with too much cream. I presumed him to be one of the Vlad clan.

As the vampire continued his work, he reached up for a book on a shelf. The book was back too far, and he had to shift his body more to reach it. That's when I noticed he was in a wheelchair. Suddenly the end of a crutch bumped the top of the book, and it fell into the mustached vampire's hands. "Thank you, my dear," his mature baritone voice murmured.

"Hard work, easy work, with teamwork. That's what we do, work, work, work," said the top-heavy, pale, blue-eyed, young lady with the skin so creamy and pale she looked like freshly poured milk.

Although she used crutches, she walked with a fluid grace that made her sandy-blonde hair flow from side to side.

"If I didn't know better, I would think she is flirting with him," I said to myself. The idea of two Keepers dating was illegal. The thought of two physically disabled getting together and having an even more disabled child was punishable by death of the child and the parents. Then a thought came to my mind—a thought that had never occurred to me in my entire existence. "If it was illegal for the disabled to have children, then where did disabled babies come from? I mean, I know where babies come from, but where did the disabled ones come from?" I murmured to myself a little too loud.

"Who's there?" the mustached vampire shouted.

I maneuvered around the window to hide, then decided to walk in the door. If the Enthol were called, I would be on the run again. I was too hungry and weak to run.

"I am sorry to bother you. I mean no harm. I am in dire need of a computer." I entered the room with my head bowed, and my arms stretched out as a sign of surrender.

"Who are you? What are you wearing?" Mustache asked.

"Look at his arm; he is one of us." Blondie smiled as she cautiously walked toward me. "From which library do you hail? You dress like a homeless human. Oh, goodness! You smell awful," she said, putting a hand over her nose and mouth and slowly backing away.

"Sorry I was—I have been out of sorts lately. One of the reasons I need to use your computer." I pressed the issue.

"If you are one of us, tell me, what library are you from?" Mustache inquired

"My name is Zarian Kane. Please, let me use your computer, and I will tell you all you want to know. I don't know how much longer I have here. I must find out who is trying to kill me and why," I explained.

"You lie; Zarian Kane committed treason, and we killed him running from the Enthol," Blondie shouted while blocking me from further entering the room.

"I don't have time for this! Move out of my way!" I was prepared to shove my way through when they moved aside on their own.

Their eyes hazed over; immediately I could tell that I had control over them. I did not mean to control them, nor did I wish to keep control over them, but I needed that computer. I fumbled past them and sat at the computer.

I tried to log on to the computer, but my access had been locked out. I was about to attempt to hack through mentally; then I thought, *If I try to mentally log on, I may be discovered.*

"If I try to log in mentally, I may lose control of these two and more problems will follow," I whispered out loud.

"How do I get access to the Sharuk when my login has been removed" I murmured to myself.

"We will log you in," both vampires answered in unison.

I looked up and across to them. I had forgotten they were still in a trance. I had even forgotten they were Keepers. I had forgotten they were also there. They made a valid point; both had access to the Sharuk.

53

"How did I forget them? They are standing right here," I said to myself, yet speaking out load.

"Sir, would you please log in to the Sharuk archive program?" I said to the mustached Keeper.

"My name is Lou Verod," he replied.

I was taken aback by this; was he still under my control? I thought, *I did not ask for your name.*

"You did not, but I sensed you were calling me Mustache. Although my mustache is extraordinarily handsome, it does not define who I am," he said.

"Okay, Mr. Verod, would you mind logging on to the Sharuk?" I calmly asked, wondering why he had some sense of free will even though he was in a trance.

"I would mind if I had a choice! Even though my words are my own, I cannot stop myself from doing your bidding."

"I cannot express to you how sorry I am for putting you through this. If it were not life or death, I would never invade you in such an intrusive way," I said as I crouched behind him to get a good view of the computer.

For a moment there was a pause, as Mr. Verod entered the archive of the Sharuk.

A mental wave glitched across the computer. Someone was trying to block me, but their power was nothing compared to my new-found strengths. I felt myself getting weaker. I urged Mr. Verod to hurry.

As we feverishly scrolled through page after page of documentation, we started noticing discrepancies. The first was the growing number of disappearances and deaths of infant vampires. The second discrepancy was the bloodline of ancestors; there were more Ancient Ones than initially thought. These Ancient Ones were not spoken of by their names. This made it difficult to create an accurate archive of them. They were called the Feral Ones.

54

The Feral Ones were the first to realize that the hunger they suffered could be satisfied best by drinking blood, any blood. They found that human blood could sustain them longer.

They secretly, fiendishly, realized that eating the flesh of other vampires gave them special abilities. The stronger the consumed vampire, the more power and abilities the Feral Ones gained.

With the new powers and abilities came some strange side effects. The first change was the effect of the sun on them. The changes started slowly: sunburns after short periods in the sun. Eventually, after consuming more power, the Feral Ones would burst into flames with the hint of sunlight.

When the Ancient Ones realized the horrors, they set out to destroy the Feral Ones. The Feral Ones merged their power and formed a rift in space. They created a hiding place, a parallel world to the mortal one.

The adverse effect of the sun, then adding prolonged travel in the parallel world caused the Feral Ones' pupil and iris to switch, causing a change how light is viewed in the light spectrum.

More documents showed that for thousands of years the vampire world grew equal but separate from the mortal world—soon to be called the human world, named after the dominant species of that realm. The remaining vampires eventually died out or were killed.

For hours, we searched through the Sharuk, and more and more anomalies were discovered. Another hidden file showed the Feral Ones were not the only vampires to leave the mortal world. Many of the weaker vampires were captured and forced to serve the Feral Ones.

The Feral Ones bred with their servants and had offspring with them. These children would have genetic traits of both their parents. The combination of these genes would sometimes cause the child to have limbs and digits deformed.

Verod looked up at Zarian. "The Sharuk talks about the Ancient Ancestors as the first vampires. If they were brought here as slaves, what happened to the Feral Ones? These were files hidden in the Sharuk. I don't think we were meant to see this. Then again, someone put the files in here for someone to find—eventually, right?"

Suddenly the computer screen started flashing red and locked up.

"They are on to you," Verod said, blankly staring at me.

"You, Blondie, get me a recording device," I said in my most intimidating gangster voice. I don't think it went over as well as I hoped.

"My name is Mina Montz, not Blondie," she grunted as she went over to the counter and began setting up monitors and recorders.

"Sorry, Miss Montz, I am not ordinarily such a pompous jerk. This is kind of a life or death situation, and candor at this point is a necessity," I said, giving her a small bow. I proceeded to position myself in front of where the cameras were being set up.

As the camera started, I began to speak. "Hello, my name is Zarian. I don't have much time to talk to you; it's dusk, and they will be coming soon. I am sending this video to you in hopes that in my death, the truth will come to light. The traitor is far beyond my bounds, and I am but one who could not think of opposing such power. But you can! I know that when you see the evidence that I have brought forth, you will put a stop to the killings and bring forth justice."

56

I released my control over my fellow Keepers. I was hoping they would stop the cameras. I was hoping they would flee and leave me, but they didn't.

That was when I realized the truth in the situation. The Keepers were not in my control, nor had they ever been. They were playing along to see what the rogue Keeper would do.

Verod looked up toward me with a sneer on his face. "How could you come in here, dressed like a buffoon, and pretend you are the Zarian Kane."

"But I am Zarian Kane. The Enthol are after me still. I did not die, but I fear my death is at the top of someone's agenda," I explained, utterly embarrassed by their ruse.

"You have seen the evidence for yourselves; someone is covering up the truth of the vampire world and how we came to be," I shouted. I was really getting tired of being the dumbest one in the room.

57

"Zarian Kane has been dead for two years. Everything he had ever touched was destroyed: his home, his friends, his co-workers, they even burned down his library." Mina lurched forward to strike, remembered the smell, and decided to stand her ground.

"Wait, did you say two years? I was in the human world for two or three nights. I fell asleep in the sewer and woke up the next night." I was confused and getting scared. How could a vampire live for two years without blood?

"Don't you think we Keepers have suffered enough? Why stir up his memory and cause our people more harm? Verod exclaimed.

"Your people?" I questioned.

"Yes, after Zarian died and they started killing the Keepers that knew him; we started to realize how many of us there really were. We started a communication link with each other, and we started to form groups. We needed to try to make escape plans to avoid the genocide," Verod said, popping a wheelie and maneuvering himself around the camera setup to face me.

I felt the light of dawn start to creep its way into the sky. Then a loud sound echoed through the library.

"This is the Enthol. You have a fugitive vampire in your domain. You have only a few minutes until dawn. If you don't send him out, we will come in and bring everyone inside out into the light! You have one minute!" the Enthol shouted over an intercom.

"I told you!" I smirked. I got up and headed for the door.

"Where are you going?" Mina asked, watching me straightening out my clothes.

"I believe what you said about all the deaths of my friends. No one else needs to die because they know me. In case the Enthol decide to burn this library down, could you please send the video to the other libraries or anyone who you think would listen? Don't let the deaths of my friends, my family of Keepers be in vain."

I let them watch my smirk fade as I walked to the door. To be honest, I had hoped to look brave as I made my way across the room to the door. The distance got longer and longer, and my feet got heavy, I choked back a tear and clenched my fists as I tried to stave off my fear.

I opened the door and saw that dawn was almost here. I shielded my eyes from the rays that peered over the horizon. The air was already starting to get hot. The cold chill down my spine now had the warmth of sunburn.

Then everything was dark again. I blinked a few times to get my bearing. Was I dead? I didn't feel dead. But then again, what does feeling dead actually feel like? I looked around and recognized the familiar surroundings. I was back in the sewer.

Now I knew there were at least two entities at play or playing with me. Someone was trying to help me find the truth, and someone was trying to have me killed. The first was powerful enough to transport me from the vampire world to the human world. The other was powerful enough to transport me back to the vampire world and plop me down in front of the Enthol Headquarters.

"What do they want from me? I am just a Keeper; I am harmless, my friends were harmless," I said as I sat in the sewer, waiting for the night to fall.

"Maybe I don't know what I know," I said, trying to figure out how I got into this situation.

"What do I know? There were two powerful vampires with an agenda. There were discrepancies in the Sharuk. Everyone had forgotten all knowledge of the Feral Ones, but how? How could anyone forget their parents or grandparents? How are there no stories or records? How did we not know that we all were part of the human world at some point in time?" My head hurt. I was hungry before; now I was starving.

"It will be hours before sunset. I don't know how I have lasted this long," I mumbled out loud and lay down for a rest.

[Flash of bright red]

"Silly boy. So many hints and you still can't figure the riddle." A woman's voice washed over me like a raging river on a hot summer night. It surrounded me, crashed into me. I felt the sensation of drowning in her power.

Out of the darkness, her eyes appeared. Her pupils were blood red. The thing I found most disturbing was that her eyes seemed to smile at me. The smile was not that of cheer; it was more like a predator playing with its food.

"So, boy, tell me; what have you learned?" she inquired, as if she already knew the answer.

"I learned that there were vampires before the Ancient Ones. They were called the Feral Ones," I responded

"Wrong!" she shouted at me. "The Ancient Ones did not come to the vampire world. The Feral Ones and their slaves did."

I paused and pondered this for a while.

"The Sharuk was changed to make it seem like the Ancient Ones came to the vampire world. Then erased all traces of the Feral Ones and made the slaves seem as if they were the Ancient Ones."

"You are getting closer, child," the voice in my head said.

"Who are you?" I asked.

"You were doing so well; now you have lost focus again or did you?" the voice sighed.

61

[Flash of bright red]

The Queen, Lie`t `at Ravvi le Drak continued to sit on that spot on the floor long after Ravvi the Drak went to slumber. As the sun rose, she continued to sit. As a beam of sunlight found a crack in the window covering and began to burn her skin, she continued to sit. As her clothing charred and her flesh began to burn away, she continued to sit when the smoke alarm sounded, and the Gray Guard covered her with a shielding cloak. She continued to sit on that spot on the floor. The Gray Guard tried to move their queen to safety. And could not. There was a force, a power holding her to that spot.

"Alert the king! The queen is in danger," Blake ordered. "We are under attack."

"Yes, sir!" a guard replied. "Sir, who are we under attack from?"

"I don't know, but this is the second attack in two years. We have a traitor in the castle," Blake answered.

[Flash of bright red]

"Young one, my time here is almost over. In my rage, I let down my guard, and my punishment will not be swift." The voice spoke with sadness.

"Are you my mother?" I asked

"No, child. So, close yet so far. I can hear your wheels turning. I can smell my flesh burning. My heart is no longer yearning. Their control is most concerning." The voice continued as our link started to fade.

"You have been in a trance for two years, yet you live, child. You do not need blood to survive. None of us do. That is secret, number one. You must stop the war be-." Then she was gone.

I awoke in the darkness of the sewer. From the looks of the utility hole cover, I could tell I was in the human world.

Despite all that was happening, the only thing I could think of was "Lilly!" I shouted.

I climbed out of the sewer. I was dirty, ragged, tired, and I smelled like—well, I smelled like I just came out of a sewer.

"At least I am in human clothes, so that is one less thing to dread." I sighed.

It was night, not too late; maybe around seven o'clock. "If Lilly is at work, I can sneak into her apartment and borrow clothes and clean up," I planned.

I made my way through the city, trying my best to avoid any well-lit areas.

"The Enthol almost had me. I do not believe I will have my guardian angel to protect me if I am cornered again. I have to be more vigilant," I murmured under my breath as I walked past two old men drinking beside an old tree.

My fangs began to grow as I drew near. I almost started to salivate, thinking of how delicious and warm their blood would taste. Then I remembered what the voice said. I did not have to drink blood to feed.

I needed to feed. The voice told me I did not need to feed on blood.

"How am I supposed to survive without feeding?" I whispered.

"Hey buddy, want a drink?" one of the men chuckled.

"I most definitely do," I said. I thought as I drew near that these men had no idea they would be the drink.

I got closer to the two men and could tell that they were home-less. I could also tell that they had been drinking for a while. Standing beside them, it appeared we were wearing the same cologne.

The host of the little gathering smiled.

"Getting kinda chilly out here." His missing front teeth enhanced his strong southern accent and made his voice roll through his drunken stupor.

The old geezer to the left of my host handed me a bottle wrapped in a bag. I almost smiled at the cliché I was experiencing. I reached out to grab the bottle and felt a spark. It was a small zap or twinge where our fingers touched. I jeered and stepped backward. When I looked up at the old man, I could tell he was as surprised as I was.

"The imbalance of electric charge on or in the surface material is called static electricity," the old geezer responded while adjusting his cracked-lensed glasses. His hands, although visibly shaking, still held the bottle.

"Uh—a little dizzy. Pass me the bottle," the host whimpered, stumbling closer to the trashcan fire.

64

I looked up and saw these black spots and squiggly lines floating toward me like objects floating in a river.

As each object touched my skin, I felt a little stronger. The old geezer took off his glasses and dropped to his knees. I took a deep breath, which I soon regretted, and decided to walk away.

Another precious hour had passed, and I was at the door of Lilly's apartment. I jiggled the handle with the naive hope that the door would miraculously open.

A woman with a thick accent shouted, "Get the doe fo' me."

The door flung open abruptly. A young dark-skinned man, around six feet tall, opened the door. He was wearing oval-shaped glasses that possibly made him look younger than he was. His hair was like thick black sheep's wool, twisted into little jagged points all over his head. The result was that his hair looked like a porcupine was sitting on his head.

In the background, a middle-aged black lady saw me and shuffled toward the door. Her smooth black hair was pulled back in a bun. She wore black slacks and a blue short-sleeved blouse. The yellow and green checkered apron around her waist seemed to personify that she was a businesswoman, who knew her way around a kitchen.

I duck my head down a little and exaggerated my misshapen form.

"Thorry, toe thorry. I looking fo my frin, Lilly," I mumbled, trying the "I am a helpless handicapped man" skit again.

"Ya look like ya had a little bit of trouble, child. Come on inside; looks like you need you a washrag and a sandwich. Come in, child, let's get you fixed up," she said with a smile that was a little too warm and welcoming.

The young man closed and locked the door behind me.

I looked up and gave a half smile back to the welcoming lady. "Where is Lilly?" I asked.

"**Y**ou kin stop tha lil ruse, Zarian. We've been here fa near two years wait'n for you to show up. Child, we was aw ready to give up; then you showed up at the master library and renewed our faith in yo stupidity," she said.

The young man's youthful expression faded away as he crossed to the other side of me. Dread chilled every part of me like a winter cold.

The woman continued to smile as a long spear-shaped object appeared from behind her back. It pulsed with sparkling light as she brought it to her side and got into a defensive posture.

"Your choice, child. Alive or dead, we don't care, but your crazy antics gonna stop here today—the how part, that's up to you. On a personal note, I wanna see what all dat fuss is about. You haven't gone up against a real vampire—have you?" She smiled like the Cheshire cat, baiting me to attack her.

Her teammate was behind me again. He was deathly still and deadly silent. He was a full vampire. I could instinctively tell.

"Where is Lilly?" I demanded.

Then I was struck from behind, and my head cracked the tile floor. In a haze, I staggered to my feet.

"This isn't your house; it is Lilly's. You have no power here," I whispered, feeling anger well up in my voice.

"Wrong on SO many levels, child. She ain't lived here in years."
The woman laughed.

Then a blow to the side of my head spun me, and I hit the floor
hard. It became apparent that this guy was a vampire of few words.

"We are the owners of this domicile, child. Therefore, the power
of the threshold does not apply here." She laughed.

Then I laughed. "The rule of the threshold is for humans, not vampires. We are equal here," I said, shaking as I began to get to my feet.

I saw stars, not the flashes of white. Instead, it was the black spots
and wiggly lines.

These lines were not as thick as the ones with the old geezers. I
could feel myself getting stronger as they flowed near me, no—they
floated into me.

The sneaky partner tried to kick me as I was getting up; I was
faster. His foot missed, and he lost his balance.

The woman saw this and turned; her smile turned into a sneer. She swung her weapon at me. She missed also.

I took a deep breath, and the wiggles started to flow toward me faster. The black specks were coming from the two vampires as they positioned themselves for a more coordinated attack.

I could not tell if they were moving slower or if I was moving faster. The tide had changed with each second as I was able to dodge the attacks more and more efficiently.

I finally realized that I was absorbing the black specks and they were giving me energy. I was drawing the power from my attackers, and they were starting to feel it.

"Why am I so slow?" I asked, as it dawned on me what the voice was saying.

The two attackers either did not realize the seriousness of their situation, or more likely, their egos prevented them from seeing the danger. Their overconfidence was my gain.

I felt my strength returning. I felt more than my strength; it was like a deep primal strength. With this new strength, I had one thought that vibrated through my entire vampire existence. "TEACH THEM RESPECT!"

My attackers regained their composure and positioned themselves to strike.

I spoke out in a voice that even I barely recognized as my own. "Sit down!"

To my surprise, the two vampires sat down. They immediately flopped down on the floor like obedient dogs. I saw in their eyes that they were as surprised as I was.

"What just happened? What did you do to me, child? Why can't I move?" the woman shouted.

It was at that moment I recognized her voice. She was one of the Enthols that made newscasts on the computers.

She had been in the human world for so long that she had picked up a weird Haitian, Asian-like accent. Her surprised, wide eyes revealed the contacts vampires use to disguise our eyes. For the moment, they were on the floor, seemingly under my control.

As she sat there demanding, I answer her questions. I had a few questions of my own. Besides, I had no idea how to answer her questions, but I would not tell them this.

It is time for me to take charge of this situation, I thought to myself. I leaned in close to the woman and got so close I could smell the blood from her last meal.

"Where is Lilly?" I demanded.

The woman turned her head from me, trying not to answer or maybe my stench was getting to her. "She moved to Atlanta. We wiped her mind clean of the events that came from yo lil visit, child."

"Do not call me child again. It sounds condescending and undignified!" I growled at her. "Why would you wipe her mind instead of killing her?" I paused. "I mean, I am glad that you did not kill her, but why didn't you kill her?" I started babbling.

"Oh, chiii—" the word got caught in her throat and started choking her. "If we killed her and you found out, the trap wouldn't have worked. If you found out she had moved, we had a trap set up in Atlanta also."

"That is a well thought out plan. Who came up with this plan?" I asked as I knelt beside her.

"We thought of it together. We are one, but we are many, chii—" she said, choking on her words again, this time it seemed more painful.

I thought, *I guess she really cannot help saying, child. It's part of her personality, not a show of disrespect.* "You can say child again. In return, I want to know who is trying to kill me and why."

"Chiii, child, all I know is the Congregation Council are not in charge of the council. It is governed by a group of much older, much, much stronger vampires. They have huge power, and they work as one. Most importantly, they want you dead, and so we, the Enthol, will abide." Her head tilted up with pride and defiance.

68

"Well, child," I said, childishly mocking her. "I have gathered some information about the Ancient Ones. Did you know that the Ancient Ones were not that ancient? The vampires we refer to as the Ancient Ones were brought to the vampire world as slaves for the Feral Ones. The Feral Ones created the vampire world because they were eating humans and vampires." I sneered as I explained the truth of our existence to my attackers.

The little black specks continued to flow, and I noticed her eyes and skin tone had begun to lose their luster. Her dark chocolate skin had started to look ashen and dry. It was evident she was losing her focus.

"Stay with me; I need you to tell me where they are. Where can I find your Ancient Ones?" I pressed her, seeing that I was losing her, and I did not know how to turn the black speckles off.

"I don't know; we have not been in the vampire world in over fifty years. They tell us what they want, and we do it. Period!" she replied in a sleepy, dreamlike tone.

"What about you, sir? What can you tell me?" I sneered in frustration as I turned toward the other attacker.

It was at that time I became bone-chilling afraid. The male attacker was staring at me blankly as if he were in a trance. He was being drained like the female vampire, but he was showing no signs. He was staring and listening. I could tell that he was not, really there.

I swallowed a lump in my throat as my ego faded. "Who are you? Why are you trying to kill me?"

The woman laughed as if in a haze. "Oh child, he doesn't talk. Think of him like a surveillance camera. If the Ancient Ones watched through me as I did their bidding, then they would see only my point of view. With him, they can watch me and my objective," she explained. "While you were pumping me for information, we were collecting intel on how much you . . . you knew." She said as she passed out.

I turned to the young male vampire; his deep dark ebony skin was getting the ashen hue now. His gaze never changed. Whoever was controlling this puppet was going to watch until the end.

Then it dawned on me. Why was I so slow! They were watching, and reinforcements were coming if they weren't already here. And here I was sitting around like an idiot, again.

"Time to go," I said out loud, then smacked myself on the forehead with my palm. *Stop telling the people who are trying to kill you what your intentions are*, I thought to myself.

I walked out the door and looked down at my sweatshirt. There was a clump of something yucky on my shirt. I brushed at it with my sleeve, and that area came clean. The dirt and yuck flaked off with ease. I swiped at another spot; more flakes came off, leaving behind more clean areas. For the next minute or so, I flicked and swiped until I was not only clean, but I was refreshed.

I sighed. "I wish I'd known how to do that earlier. I was starting to get a headache from the stench," I murmured to myself.

70

If I stayed away from Lilly, she should be safe, I hope, I thought. *For now, I must find a way to fight the Ancient Ones, whom I believe are the Feral Ones or at least they are pulling the strings. The Feral Ones are way too powerful for me to take on.* I sat in the hallway of Lilly's old apartment, afraid of going outside.

"The last time I went outside after being found by the Enthol, it was almost fatal."

I sighed as I sat there in the hall. "There are only a few hours until dawn. I must find a resting place. I had to devise a plan. If I could not be stronger than my enemy, then I must be smarter. Yeah, good luck with that!" I sarcastically said to myself.

There I was in the hallway, asleep. I woke up with the sun shining in my face. The sunlight tingled and itched, sort of like a prickly bug crawling on my skin; of course, I did not realize this at the beginning.

Upon opening my eyes and seeing the sun, I screamed bloody murder and tried to squeeze myself into a shaded corner.

It took me a few moments of screaming to realize I was not burning. It took a few moments more to realize that no one came out of their rooms to investigate the commotion.

I gazed around the hallway in amazement. The sunlight was beautiful. Then, I saw them again—the pesky little black squiggles. They were coming from everywhere now, from the floor, the doors of the other apartments, and the walls and ceiling. The little squiggles were all around me, in me, washing over me.

They were keeping the sun from destroying me but allowing me to feel the glory of the light, and I was grateful, and so I said it out loud.

"Thank you, little squiggly speck things. I do not know how long I will live with the Feral Ones and the Enthols after me, but to be able to feel the sun and bath in its beauty was a gift I could never repay." I humbly spoke out loud.

In what seemed like thousands of little voices, whispering precisely in the same instance, I heard "You're welcome." The voice or sound was not heard in my head or my ear; it was more like it washed over me, in and around me. I knew it was them.

71

"What are you? Sorry, I don't mean to sound rude, but this is beyond incredible." I was hyperventilating with excitement.

"We are the Darkness. Without us, there would be no life. We give essence to the life force of all living things. Thousands of years ago, all creatures lived together in harmony. All living things existed with us and us with them. Man was the caretaker of the land; soon he had sons and divided the responsibilities among them.

"One son took care of plants and vegetation. The other son was caretaker of all the animals. One day man killed a man; he drank his essence. It made him strong." The voice of the Darkness seemed to sigh as if they remembered the event as if it were yesterday.

"The vampires you refer to as the Feral Ones started here. He soon found other creatures to serve him. Together these creatures attempted to take more essence. First, they killed animals. Together they absorbed essences and gained power, but not like that from man.

"These Feral Ones became addicted to the power of the essence, so they tried to kill the humans in Eden. We forced them away by draining their life force whenever the Feral Ones came near the human dwellings."

"Are you saying that you kept Adam and Eve from being eaten by vampires?" I asked, teetering on the cusp of disbelief.

"That is a story for a different time. The knowledge we are bestowing upon you is the reason why vampires no longer have the ability to walk in the day," the Darkness continued.

There was a long and uncomfortable pause, and I was not sure if the Darkness was going to finish.

"We are a peaceful existence. We were here before the beginning, and we will be here after the end," the Darkness continued.

"Watching how these creatures took our gift, converted it, and used it to harm others caused emotions we had never felt before. We decide the best thing for us was to remove ourselves from the Feral Ones." The Darkness seemed almost sad as it continued.

"Some Feral Ones realized the path they were on was not a good one. They set on a path to do no further harm. These vampires dedicated their life to make amends for their deeds.

"The others, the ones you refer to as the Feral Ones. They sought no redemption. They instead tried to achieve more power and attempted to control the Darkness. Their goal was to manipulate us with their power.

"By pushing us away, the light became too intense, and they burst into flames. This act was irreversible." With what seems like a chuckle, they said, "They became the first creatures of the night."

I interrupted the voice or voices to ask what I assumed was a legitimate question. "Pardon me, um, Darkness people or things. Why me? Why am I being pulled into your confrontation with the Feral Ones? I am not the best choice for championing your cause."

"You are exactly what we are looking for. Your entire existence has revolved around you being trained to do what you were told, but you have always had the free will to ask why. Which meant you were not completely under the control of the Feral Ones," the Darkness explained

"What are you saying? Are you telling me that we are all under some trance?" I asked, although I already knew the answer. I could control other vampires, but their free will was only partially taken, meaning someone or something was commanding the other part of their mind. "If I, being one of the weaker vampires, could do this, then there is no limit to what the Feral Ones could do." I let out a depressed sigh. "You should choose someone better, stronger."

"Our CHOICE, as you say, is correct," the Darkness replied, with a twinge of something in its voice that could have been aggravation.

The Darkness paused, then continued. "The Feral Ones have enslaved and controlled your kind for centuries. This abuse must come to an end. We chose you, not because of your physical or mental capabilities; we saw the strength of your heart. You desire to be a better vampire, and you did not let your disabilities dictate your ability."

The voice paused again. "Look around you, Zarian Kane. You are a vampire in the sunlight. It has been over two years since you drank blood. If there is more convincing of our power you need, maybe you were not the best choice."

"I will try my best to serve you," I humbly said as I made a small bow. "I think the Feral Ones are manipulating the so-called Ancient Ones in the vampire world. Take us there, and together we can locate them," I said with revived energy.

"This is the one thing we cannot do. The Feral Ones made the vampire world with their twisted power. It is not natural to this world; therefore, we cannot pass into it," the Darkness voiced.

"So, the Feral Ones made a power of threshold barrier against you," I stated. I had begun to chuckle, then thought better of it.

"I do not know how to get to the vampire world. Somehow, I was pulled there. Come to think of it, I was pulled here, too. Did you do that?" I asked.

"We did not send you there, but one of our dedicated servants brought you here. We have not been able to sense her. We fear she is no longer with us. The Feral Ones are creatures of habit. Once they sense we are no longer with you, they will pull you back."

I interrupted. "If you leave, they will kill me! Then you will not be able to get to the vampire world."

"Be at ease," the Darkness said. "We are with you and shall remain so. We have been flowing in and through you for the last two years. You are now part of this world again, which is why you can survive in the sun. When night falls, the Feral Ones will come for you. They will bring you back to their world. We will be ready." Then there was an abnormal silence.

"Hello, friend," a calm voice called from a corner of the room.
Although the voice spoke calmly, I was startled by the super silence in the hallway, the street, everywhere. It felt like there was a vacuum that removed all sound.

"Be at ease; we are here to help. We few that are remaining are here to stop the bad ones," it said.

I looked, and at first glance, I thought it was a combination of the human musical artists David Bowie and Billy Idol. Of course, it was not them or the combination of them. This was one of the True Ancient Ones.

I could tell it was neither male nor female because the sheer robe it wore revealed all, as it walked across the sunlit hall.

"How have you lived among humans so long and not been exploited?" I questioned.

They were not the average human. They had some similarities to vampires from the vampire world. They had the fangs, a tall, slender body, and reversed eyes. There were some other differences, besides being sexless, that was obvious also.

Their skin was so thin and pale, the muscle and veins were slightly visible.

"We have survived because we must," the True Ancient One

explained. "There have been times when a human has seen one of us, but their comprehension of the encounter is beyond them. Most humans say they have seen a ghost or mirage. There were some rare occasions when we had to wipe the memory of the human—not to protect us, but to help the human maintain their sanity." The Ancient One gazed around the hall.

"These are tales for a different time. There is much for you to learn about who you really are, Zarian Kane. Your time is growing short. Soon the Enthol will be here to collect your body. When they find you alive, they will alert the.... What did you call them? Oh yes, the Feral Ones." The True Ancient One tilted his head and smiled a little. It was apparent he was trying to put me at ease.

"When the Feral Ones become aware that you are alive, they will pull you back again. Be mindful that they have lived for centuries; they are no fools."

W e went into the apartment adjacent to Lilly's. The Enthol somehow evacuated the entire building.

While we waited, the True Ancient Ones taught me how to pull
the life force from all living creatures. They told me it was possible to
take just enough to make the victim tired, and not kill them. They also
told me that I could use the power in reverse and revitalize myself and
others.

Then I noticed the weirdest thing. As I was talking to the True
Ancient One, I realized we were not alone. There were other True
Ancient Ones in the room. I could sense them, I could see them out
the corner of my eye, but when I turned to look at one of them. They
were not there.

"Yes Zarian, we are ALL here," the Ancient One said.

"Why can't I see you?" I worriedly asked.

"You are a few generations removed from your ancestors. We feel
that you may not be able to comprehend what you see. It would be
foolish to test out this theory right before a battle. What you see is a
cloaked version of who we really are. After the battle is won and you
truly desire to see us, we will grant your request."

76

Like clockwork, as the sun started to set, four Enthol enforcers strolled into the hallway. Behind the door of the adjacent apartment, I crouched down and made my breath shallow. I feared that they might hear my breathing and ruin the plan.

Two of the Enthol stood guard outside. The other two entered Lilly's apartment and saw my vampire attackers still incapacitated. With a thought, the Enthol reported their findings to the Feral Ones. A second later, I was in the world of the vampire again.

That's when I started to panic. I looked around and saw that I was in front of the Enthol Headquarters again. I turned to run for cover; then I saw it. It was barely a flicker, but it was there in the fading light of the sunset. The Darkness somehow made it through.

I held up my hand to touch it and saw more pouring from my skin.

"Feed," the Darkness commanded

So, I did—I started drawing energy from everywhere and everything, just like they taught me. I absorbed the energy into myself. I felt how the land was formed from the conversion of the Darkness' power. It started to make me queasy. My vision was blurry. I looked to my right, and I saw the Darkness spinning and creating a vortex. A second later, one of the True Ancient Ones stepped through the vortex. More of the True Ancient Ones blurred through.

"Zarian send the force into the air. Let this world know the power you possess," the True Ancient Ones shouted.

77

The Ancient Ones commanded, and I was more than happy to oblige. I raised my good hand to the sky; with my other arm I gripped my belly the best I could to keep from throwing up.

From the palm of my dominant hand, a swirl of gray squiggly specks flowed.

I started to feel better as I expelled the gray force from my body. I felt the tether of the human world and began to draw power from it. The energy felt unbelievably good.

The beacon obviously worked, because the Enthol rushed out like a kicked-over ant hill. Fangs, claws, and weapons flashed around me. The True Ancient Ones were gone, which was a little off-putting. This time, I had confidence in my new teammates. I clenched my fist to my side and prepared to fight.

A calm breeze flowed through the air, trickling over me like warm honey when the breeze stopped. I was standing alone; the Enthol were all lying on the ground. I was not sure if they were alive or dead.

I did not get the chance to ask, as I prepared to check for signs of life. I was struck hard by what seemed to be the wind itself.

"Traitor, back in my day, when a child was born with a deformity, we would put it on a mountain and leave it to die," a voice said in my head. The power was as strong as the True Ancient Ones, and I knew that it was the voice of the Feral Ones.

Like the True Ancient Ones, the Feral Ones spoke as one. I could not help but wonder if seeing them would be to my detriment, as it would be if I looked upon the True Ancient Ones.

"I see you have met our jailer. Why would you side with the very beings that imprisoned us? Is your brain as twisted as your body?" the Feral Ones asked, as if they were sincere.

It would have been believable, if its tone wasn't so demeaning. From its voice-?

No, not its voice, his voice. The Feral One that was speaking was a male voice. Even though I could not see him yet, I could tell it was a male.

"You mock me. You demean and oppress me, and everyone like me. Yet here I am. Standing up to you—unafraid." I exhaled the last part, letting the words linger in the stillness of the night.

78

From the corner of my eye, I saw him. He was magnificent, in a scary way, as I was looking at him. I was at a loss for words to describe him. I think it would be easier to describe the shape and color of the air we breathe.

The power of the Feral One was beyond me, even though I was talking a good game. I was frozen to the spot. A chill slithered up my spine as I saw from the corner of my eye an image coming into focus. My mental wheels started turning as I was trying to understand the image as it was coming into focus.

Tears started to form, and my breath was getting heavy. The air was getting thick.

Brown—that was all I could comprehend right now. A brown humanoid shape. A brown, humanoid, slender form.

"I don't want to see; I don't want to see," I said to myself or maybe out loud. I did not know.

"Eyes open, eyes closed, does not matter. Death is coming for you. I am coming for you," the Feral One said.

"No, you will not bully me anymore." I craned my neck around so that I was looking directly at him.

Something snapped inside me. At first, I thought I had lost my mind. I figured my brain could not accept the image, so it created a picture I could understand. Whatever the event, I saw the Feral One.

He had a slight limp to his walk. His jawline was slanted slightly to the right. His left eye was a little larger and higher than the right one. His back had a noticeable hump.

That's when I realized—it was not an image my brain created. It was the pure form of the Feral One.

"Through all of your degradation, oppressing us to be only Keepers. You are just one of us," I sneered in disgust.

"How dare you speak to me this way? You are barely a vampire. I am your god," he said.

I laughed. Yes, I laughed at him. "I have met those with god-like powers. You are not one of them. They taught me some things. Want to see a trick?"

79

He rushed toward me with his claws out. I summoned the power, like the Darkness taught me. Then I forced it out of my hand and into the Feral One. The Feral One flew across the street and slammed into the wall of the Enthol building.

In a flash, he was up and charging for me again. I tried to throw him back again, but the first blast drained too much power. I was not absorbing the life force fast enough. If I tried to absorb more quickly, I might accidentally kill something or someone.

The Feral One pushed through the fading blast and was moving faster. This time, instead of trying to blast him away, I pulled power toward me. I pulled his power toward me. I pulled the Ancient life force out of him. I was going to absorb it into myself and replenish my energy, but his power felt wrong. I could not afford to get queasy like I did before.

"You power is an abomination to all creation. No one should possess this evil," I said as I flung my dominant hand toward the sky. Brown speckles flowed skyward and were soon joined by the gray speckles from earlier.

The vampire world started to flicker and blur in and out of focus. I dropped to my knees, drained from the battle.

"Our turn," a voice called out from behind me. It was the True Ancient One.

Its clothing was ragged and torn, and there were bruises on various parts of its body. What had transpired while I was occupied with the Feral One?

The Ancient One bowed its head and closed its eyes. Then it put its hands together as if to pray. The brown and gray specks became a giant tornado, whirling and spinning into an enormous funnel overhead.

I crouched down in fear that I would be blown away by this massive tornado. I prepared to put my hand over my eyes to shield them from the wind—there was no wind, but this was a windless tornado.

I grinned with amazement as I watched the funnel spin faster and faster. Suddenly the spinning stopped, and the massive tornado rushed down into the body of the Ancient One.

The Ancient One raised its hands toward the sky, and black specks and squiggles came forth like a swarm of bees.

The baby Darkness floated and flowed into everything—the trees, the ground, the buildings, and it even looked like the air was absorbing it.

80

The Darkness spoke through me. "You have done well. Only a vessel with a pure and true heart could bring us through to the vampire world. When we tried to come on our own, we were transformed into the gray matter you saw. Mindless energy trapped to do the bidding of the Feral Ones. Now it is finished."

"Not quite," the Ancient One said. "We must wake the vampires we made sleep."

"I was wondering why no one came out to investigate the events as they unfolded. So, you made everyone in the area fall asleep," I stated

"The world," the Ancient One replied.

"You made everyone in the vampire world fall asleep?" I asked in amazement.

"Ha, ha, ha. After all that has transpired here, you are still not thinking of the big picture," the Ancient One continued. "If all the vampires in the area were put to sleep, what would stop others from venturing into the area? What would happen if the battle continued out of the immediate area?"

"Wow, you put the entire vampire world to sleep? That's very impressive," I gasped.

What seemed like a sigh of frustration came from the Ancient

One's lips. "What would happen if the fight carried over into the human world?"

I sat down on the ground, pressed by the weight of the of realization. "You made all of the worlds fall asleep? All at once?"

"We," the Darkness replied. "We made the whole world fall asleep."

"You guys are amazing!" I stated.

"The Darkness said we, meaning all of us, Zarian. We all pulled power from the life force of every living thing in the world. The plan was to take enough to make all creatures sleep and keep them out of danger. It helped that the allies of the Feral Ones were asleep also,"The Ancient one slowly explained.

I would have been insulted if I thought it was on purpose. "So, what now? Do we destroy the vampire world, and all go to live in the human world?

"Maybe one day. Some concessions must be rendered before that happens. We are going to leave the vampires asleep and try to rid them of their bloodlust, like we did with you. We will educate them on the vampire truth. We will nurture this destroyed land. Revive the creatures that were abused and abandoned in this world."

The True Ancient One let out a sigh, then smiled with hope.

81

"In a few years, we will revive your fellow vampires. We will determine if they are ready to be part of one world at that time," the True Ancient One expressed with hope.

"What about those who will not conform?" I asked.

"Everyone deserves a chance to become better than they were. Like you," the Darkness interrupted.

"You have a bigger task at hand. You will not be a part of the vampire evolution. You will be required to go to the human world and become an ambassador to the coming events. You must prepare the human world. Let them know that your fellow vampires are coming in peace. Teach them of our laws and our culture so that one day we will again live in harmony."

I let out a deep breath. "That is a lot to ask of one person."

"Ask?" The Ancient One spoke louder than normal. "This is not a request. You will complete your task. Failure will mean your fellow vampires will sleep forever. For them to be genuinely free, the humans must accept them of their own free will."

I had never heard the Ancient One speak with such passion. It solidified the importance of my task. "I will not fail you or my people." I stood up and gave a humble bow.

It took nearly an hour for the Ancient Ones to make the sleeping vampires walk to their domiciles. Everyone was tucked away well before the sun rose. Even the vampires that were in the human world were brought back to the vampire world and placed in sanctuary domicile.

After a few days of rest and recovery in my new home, in my new bed, I set out to start my mission. To be honest, it was getting kind of creepy not being able to talk to anyone for the last couple of days. The Darkness and the True Ancient Ones had stopped communicating with me. I hoped it was because they too were busy training the thousands of vampires.

My first task on my mission, acquire new clothes. "I know just the place." I smiled to myself as I phased myself to the new home of my friend Lilly.

PART 2

Marsha: The First Soldier of the Dark

1

When Lilly opened the door, I expected her to jump at me with open arms and tears of joy. Instead, I got a blank stare as if she did not know me.

"Ah, they wiped your memory of me," I said out loud.

"Memories are a glimpse of your life. It cannot truly be erased; just hidden." I reached out and touched her with my nondominant arm.

She began to shrug back. When my arm touched, the hand holding the doorknob. She started to cry.

"Hello, my friend," I said with a smile.

Lilly replied, "I thought you were dead, you jerk! How could you leave me like that? Where did you go? My life was so much better without you! I didn't want to get involved, and you ruined my life!"

I stepped back; my heart was broken by her words.

"It's called venting, dummy. I don't really, mean it. Come here." She pulled me inside with a big hug.

She is my friend again, I thought. "Lilly, I need your help," I said, muffled in her sweatshirt. *How many of those things does she have?* I thought.

Just outside Lilly's door, we hugged for what seemed like forever.

"Come in. Where have you been? I thought you were dead. It has been two years. Where have you been?" she rambled on.

"I have quite the story to tell you, my friend. I will tell you everything. I want you to know the whole story so that you can make an informed decision," I said, loosening my embrace to look her in her hazel eyes.

I began to tell the tale that I learned. I started with the story of the Darkness and Marsha Ro-am. Marsha Ro-am was a quiet, well-mannered girl. She lived with her mother and father on a small farm outside the Drak kingdom. Marsha's family, like most of the vampires in the war-torn world, had to use the blood of livestock to survive. The blood of humans was a delicacy reserved for wealthy vampires.

One night, soldiers came and raided their small farm. Marsha's father tried to fight them off, but he was a farmer, not a fighter. Marsha's father valiantly died trying to protect his family. They were bound and gagged; Marsha and her mother were tossed into the back of a caged wagon. Tears streamed down her face as she watched the only home she had ever known go down in flames. Marsha and her mother were taken and forced into slave labor by the Faing clan.

Marsha was thirteen years old when she became a slave. Unable to cope with her father's death, Marsha refused to eat. Weak and useless, she was beaten and abused for entertainment. Finally, her little mind broke. She began to hear voices that no one else could hear.

The voices told Marsha about a world before vampires. The voices melted together with the pieces of Marsha's broken mind and showed her unique vampire kills. Marsha learned to get nourishment and survive without drinking blood. The voices told her to keep this skill secret.

It did not take long for the Faing to notice that the other slaves steered clear of Marsha. The Faing captors saw that Marsha did not beg for mercy when the guards lashed her for fun. She just stared at them. The prison guards stopped beating her that day; a few of the guards said they had nightmares of that stare.

To keep Marsha obedient, the guards would beat Marsha's mother. When Marsha gave the guards her stare, they hit her mother more. Marsha would look at the floor for the next year, and there on the floor was the last time she saw her mother. Beaten and broken, Marsha's mother died with her eyes open and her fists clenched, fighting to live so that her daughter would not be left alone. What the mother did not know was the only reason Marsha had not left the prison was that she did not want to leave her mother behind.

Marsha waited until sunrise and put her mother into the light. Her flesh burned with the task, but she did not flinch, she did not waver. "I will never bow to anyone, ever again," were the only words she muttered, as she curled into the corner where she and her mother slept. Marsha did not sleep; she sat and talked to the voices. She listened to their secrets and plans, waiting for the night to fall.

As the sun went into hiding, the guards came out to play. The prisoners started their daily rituals of cooking, cleaning, and getting beatings.

One of the guards joked to the other, "Hey, where's your crazy girlfriend and her mother?"

"Rumor has it that the mother did not fare so well from yesterday's—session," he responded, shrugging his shoulders and letting out a sneering smile.

Marsha appeared out of the shadows of the moonlight, and it seemed as if the darkness of night wrapped around her like a cloak. Marsha sneered a smile back at the guard, and his smile faded. The cold chills were visible as his smile melted away. She cocked her head to the side and stared at the two guards as she walked toward them. Her eyes were a crimson red so deep that they were almost black. The deep canyon of darkness swirled across her entire eye.

"Looks like your girlfriend wants to spend some time with you. I guess you are too scared to show her her place," the first guard teased, seeing the goosebumps on his fellow guard's arms. "After I show you how to put her in her place, I will be happy to go to your house and teach your woman her place too," he said with a childish giggle that came out more sinister than expected.

Not wanting to lose what little respect he had left; the second guard spoke up. "I got this!" He put a hand on the first guard's shoulder and pulled him a few steps behind.

Marsha froze in place, waiting on the guard to close in, the sneer still on her face.

"You, girl, you have work to do—there is no time for your crazy antics!" the second guard shouted to her.

Marsha continued to stand there with her head cocked to the side.

Getting a bit closer, the guard reached down for his baton. Marsha was familiar with that baton and the pain from it that came when the guard was bored. The beatings and begging for forgiveness for a wrong she did not commit were tattooed on various parts of her body. When the baton came out, Marsha did not flinch. She just stood and waited for the guard to come closer.

"Get back to work, you freak!" the guard shouted, raising the baton to strike.

Small and slender were her fingers. Frail was her posture. Strong and fierce was her resolve as she leaped forward, grabbing the baton in one hand and ripping into his stomach with the other. She reached deep into his body and shifted her hand upward.

The guard was on his tiptoes, trying to pull the small, frail demon hand from inside his body. He tried to let out a scream for help, but nothing came out. From the other guard's point of view, it looked as if he was trying to strangle the woman as he scolded her before the baton strike. It wasn't until he noticed him standing at a strange angle that he saw there was something weird going on.

"Hey, what are you doing over there? Getting service?" he said with a weak chuckle.

What was only a few seconds seemed like hours for the guard trapped in Marsha's grip. She dug around until she found her prize. When she finally reached her prize, they looked into each other's eyes. Her eyes were full of rage; his eyes were full of fear. Then she pulled, and he went limp. Blood streamed down her arm from the heart still pumping in her hand. Tempted to take a bite, she fought the urge and threw the still-beating heart to the ground.

The chuckling guard watched the horror of the event and was frozen in place. It took a moment for his training to kick in; then he screamed for backup as he rushed in a blur toward the fallen guard. Marsha was a blur of speed also. She thrust her hand forward toward the guard's chest. There was no time for him to stop. Her arm went into his chest almost to the elbow; in her hand beat his heart. His body first went rigid, then limp as she slid her arm out of him.

To her left, a group of guards with various weapons and shields formed ranks and headed toward her. Marsha stood her ground; alive or dead, she would be free tonight. She flexed her fingers and rotated her wrist while waiting for the first attack. Marsha could hear the heartbeat of the freshly fed; she could smell the blood coursing through their veins. As a gentle breeze blew by, she caught a whiff of a familiar scent around the compound in which she was imprisoned. The smell of fear was always present. Usually, it came from the poor souls held prisoner here. Not this time—this fear came from the guards. Fear flowed out of their pores and across the air, like rain washing across a plastic tarp.

6

Marsha knew that their fear could be used to her advantage. She also knew that if she made the first move, it would take away her advantage. So, she sat and waited for the guards to make their move. The guards did not move. It was like they were waiting for a command to charge, a command that did not come. She directed a piercing glare at the biggest of the group and laughed out loud.

"Such a burly beast, cowering before a little girl. Run along, let your cowardice be your punishment for your crime, not death." She waved her hand dismissively at them.

"How dare you talk to us this way, peasant!" the big guard replied to her taunt. He lunged forward to attack. A few of the guards with him charged also.

Marsha's speed was too much for them; the guards fell in heaps. Two of the four lay with their throats ripped out. Two were in a ball with blood flowing from an undeterminable area underneath them. The last of them, the big burly guard, dangled limply, his throat in the clutch of Marsha's hand. She cocked his head so that the other guards could see his face. Then she whispered something in his ear. His body immediately convulsed with fear. The horror of her words twisted his face in terror. The sight caused the remaining guards to take steps backward.

Marsha dropped the guard and took a step forward. The big guard lay in a heap as she walked by. His face was a twisted mess that tried to let out a scream but could not get it out. He just lay there and drooled, with his eyes focused on nothing. Whatever she said to him, it was like his mind could not process it.

She took another step forward, this time more assertively and with more confidence. A guard on her left stepped back and fell. She was on top of him like a blur of light. She placed her hand on his chest and then lifted it about four inches, hovering over his heart. Just beneath her hand was a shimmer, a small heatwave of energy flowing into her hand.

She looked up at her prey, which was once her captor, and smiled. "End scene. Time for act two." She stood and walked toward them.

A surge of energy coursed through her body; the guard lay dead, drained of all his life force. Seeing the events that had occurred, the remaining guards took off running. Some of the guards screamed, but most just dropped their weapons and ran away.

The other prisoners were astonished to see the little girl chase off the military-trained guardsmen. The prisoners and guards stood aside and watched as she walked right out the gate. Rumors started spreading around the local villages that prisoners had escaped too. The legend of the Death Whisper spread like wildfire.

Marsha slipped into the darkness and set up a little camp. A farmer and his son were walking through the woods and found Marsha in a home-made cave, dug under the base of a tree trunk. It was a few hours until dawn. Her body was inside the cave, but her head was sticking out of the opening. With all the foliage and at that angle, the farmer thought it was a bodiless head lying on the ground. To add to the fright factor, Marsha was staring into the night sky; she did not react as they approached.

The farmer's son, being young and curious as to why a headless vampire did not turn to ash, picked up a stick and poked Marsha in the cheek.

"Stop that." She spoke in a nonchalant tone which added to the creepiness of the scenario.

The farmer screamed a high-pitched squeal that would seem impossible to come out of the weathered old vampire. The son dropped to the floor and wet himself. It took a few minutes for the boy to regain control of his body. Meanwhile, he lay there on the ground listening to the conversation of the farmer and the young vampire whose head was attached to its body.

"Holy moly, girl, why are you in the ground like that?" the farmer shouted, in a voice way more masculine than the previous scream.

"The sun is coming up; the sun is still bad—for now," Marsha responded.

"Why don't you just go home? Can you make it there before the sun comes up?" the farmer questioned her while sizing her up, trying to get a handle on this absurd situation.

"Home is where your heart is. My heart is broken. Home is where you lay your head. I lay my head here. Here is my broken-hearted home." Then she turned and began to set up the branches beside the hole that was disturbed when she crawled out of the entrance.

"Don't you gots a mummy 'n' daddy?" the farmer's son said as he got to his feet, completely ignoring the fact that he just wet himself.

"Yes, I have parents—a mother and father. Soldiers killed them. I asked them to bring my parents back, but they said that it was not in their power. I told them I did not want to be alone. They said that they will be with me now and forever more." Marsha stopped talking and sat on the ground. She looked up at the sky and began to stare again.

The farmer took his son by the hand and began to back away from the crazy girl. The son saw a tear roll down her face.

The son looked at his father and asked, "Is she broken, Daddy?"

The farmer replied, "Yes, I think she is." He turned the boy around to walk away.

"You can fix her, Daddy; you can fix anything."

The boy smiled a little.

"I don't think I can. Some things are like broken glass; we can find all the pieces and glue them together, but it is not going to be the same," the farmer explained.

"But, Daddy, the broken things in the museum are worth something even if they are broken. Right?" The little boy was not letting the matter go, and the farmer saw this.

"Well, we could use an extra hand around the farm, and another lady around could give your ma some company." He scratched his head, trying to figure out how to invite the girl over.

"Excuse me, little lady, if you aren't busy tonight, we would like to invite you over for supper." The farmer glanced down at Marsha, who had returned to the small cave.

"I don't eat much anymore. I should have withered and died long ago, but I am still—here," she replied. "If you need someone to walk with you and make sure you get home safe, I can do that. My services are only for tonight; tomorrow I will be gone."

The farmer smiled. "Okay then, we will enjoy your company tonight and wish you farewell tomorrow."

"Great! Can we go now? I am starting to get a rash." The son sighed as the three started toward the farm, which was a secluded stretch of land off the regular path and miles from others.

Marsha ended up staying with the farmer and his family for twenty years. At the end of each night, she packed a bag as if she would be leaving the next night. Even though she learned the names of her hosts the first night she came to the farm. She still called the farmer "Farmer," she called the farmer's son "Farm Boy" or just "Boy," and farmer's wife she simply called "Ma'am." It was Marsha's ritual she would do every day, no matter how the farmer's family tried to convince her that she was welcome.

For the first ten years or so, Marsha worked the fields, fed the animals, cleaned the stalls, and helped prepare meals. When a group of invaders came, she defended the farm as if it were her own. She fought as if her life were again on the line. She was silent and deadly. The five men who dared to steal from the farm had no idea how bad the mistake they made was until it was too late.

The farmer looked out into the field where the last two invaders had fled. He saw Marsha in pursuit and chased after them. When he got there, Marsha had ripped the heart from one invader and was holding the last one by the throat.

"Stop! Please stop!" the farmer yelled

Marsha cocked her head to the side and looked at the farmer. "What did you say?"

"Please, let him go. They are just hungry and desperate," the farmer pleaded.

"If Ma'am and Boy were home alone, would they have mercy on them? No! They would destroy. It's what their kind does. They need to pay; they need to learn," she said in a low voice.

"I know that there are bad things out there, but we can't be like dem." The farmer tried to appeal to her conscience. Then realized that during the entire time she had been there, she never showed any indication that she had a conscience. She never showed any remorse for anything she had ever done.

"If you let him live, he can go back and tell others to stay away for their safety. That way we don't have to worry about more invaders. He will tell everyone to stay clear." He looked at the invader, who was nearly unconscious as he stood there with both feet flat on the ground, with his knees bent like wet noodles.

11

Marsha loosened her grip on the invader's throat. The invader started to wheeze as the air was allowed into his lungs.

"Look at me, see me!" she said to the invader. "You will tell them to stay away. You will convince them of the peril they will be in if they come here. Yes?"

"Yes," gasped the invader.

"But how will I know that you won't return with more? Oh, I know." Marsha smiled and ripped the invader's left arm off. "If I ever see you again, I will take another limb. No matter how many come, no matter If we are in passing and you mean me no ill will. I will take a limb. Do you understand?

The violent action was so fast that it took a second for the invader to realize what had happened. Marsha let him go, and he flopped on the ground in pain. She leaned down to get face to face with the invader. "Do —You — Understand? She paused between each word as she spoke through her gritted teeth.

"Yes, yes I understand." The invader panted and sobbed the words. As he looked into the emptiness of her eyes, he knew she meant every word she said.

The farmer dropped to his knees and knelt there staring with his mouth wide open. It was too much violence for him. He and his family were peaceful vampires. The only blood they drank was the blood from their livestock. They got their blood through a process they called milking. Milking was a humane way vampires got blood from animals. The milking process was minimally invasive and did not kill the animal. Even during this process, the farmer got a little woozy if the animal cried out.

The spectacle the farmer had just witnessed essentially shut his brain off. Slowly he started to regain his senses. As he began to come around, he saw Marsha sitting beside him. Marsha's hair was covering her face as she sat beside him in silence.

"My bag is packed. I will go. Thank you for trying to help me. Some things, once broken, cannot be fixed." Marsha started to stand and leave.

The farmer placed his hand on her shoulder and pulled her close and hugged her. "What you did, I fear I could never do. You protected my family. You saved the farm and us. You may be broken, but you hold great value to my family and me. Please stay."

The rumor of the Death Whisperer spread even faster. Sadly, there were some who looked at the frail appearance of the girl and saw her as a victim. Those poor souls were left to ashes or worse. For those who had witnessed the gruesome account, they reported the eerie event of the corpses staring into the distance as they turned to ash. All accounts said that she whispered something into her victim's ear. When she whispered her enchanted words, the predators who became the prey froze in place. Some she would finish off with a horrible attack, some she would just let fall to the ground. Whether the attacker was male or female, the look of horror was the same.

"You see, Lilly, Marsha, who was soon to become Queen, had absorbed the power of the Darkness. The darkness was trying to build an army by going into the vampires that attacked her. The Darkness was unsuccessful at all attempts. The experiment left the vampires in a catatonic state. From the view of the onlookers, she cast some a spell on her attackers." I paused as I watched her lean forward and gave me her undivided attention. What had she been focused on before?

Oh well—I continued. "The Darkness tried with different breeds, ages, and genders of vampires; all were unsuccessful until me. For some reason, unknown to the Darkness, the True Ancient Ones, or me, I was able to absorb the Darkness and bring them to the vampire world. The rest is history," I said as I ended my story. I looked behind me, because that was where her focus kept going. I realized that I had intruded on her night and I had been there for hours.

"I am sorry, my friend. I have interrupted your evening. Should I go?" I asked, feeling like a third wheel, although no one was here. *Was someone here?* I thought to myself. *I hope not; I just spilled the biggest secret in the world of man, if there were someone there.*

"My friend, something is bothering you. Something that is starting to cause me concern. Is there someone here? Surely you would not let me tell my tale with an outsider in the room. That would be very bad, for all of us." I frowned at her, realizing that she had not spoken the entire time since we walked into her house. "We have gone through so much, Lilly; what are you hiding from me?"

"I would not say she is hiding as much as she is protecting. I ain't sure if she's protecting you or me." A young man walked out of the shadow of a corner. His voice was deep, but barely on the verge of maturity.

"Good evening. I am Count—nah, I'm just kiddin'. My name's Gerald," he said as he strolled out into the light. "I always wanted to say that." Gerald's smile was warm and friendly.

"Sorry to eavesdrop on you, but you sure do talk a lot." Gerald's slight southern drawl made the statement more of a matter of fact rather than an insult.

I ignored the words he was saying. I could not believe there had been someone in the room for hours and I did not sense him at all. I tapped into the essence of the darkness to feel for his power. I felt nothing. I tried to absorb some of his energy, and suddenly a wave of power tossed me across the room.

"What was that?" Gerald's voice held a hint of anger. "I tried to reach out to you as a friend, and you tried to feed off of me. Bad boy! Bad, bad boy!"

"I was not trying to feed off you; I was trying to see what you are. I cannot sense you; I cannot sense you at all," I said as I stumbled to my feet.

"See with yo eyes, not with yo uh, um—you know what I'm tryna say," Gerald said, shaking his index finger at me.

"That's enough!" Lilly finally spoke up. "You are not allowed to wreck this house too." She looked over to me. "And you, this is a guest in my house; if you can't respect each other, then show me respect and leave!"

"But he started it," Gerald retorted, then frowned, realizing how childish he just sounded. "I apologize for my actions—Zarian, was it? If you behave, I will behave. Deal?"

My fangs grew longer, and my eyes flashed red. I took a deep breath and calmed down. As I reverted to normal, I let out a sigh. "I will do whatever makes you happy, Lilly, my friend."

"You say you don't have to drink blood anymore—well, Gerald doesn't drink blood either. Maybe you are related, or the same breed of Vampire or something." Lilly spoke, trying to build peace through a common ground.

"Not likely," I said

"Not possible," Gerald said, almost at the same time as me.

"If he were a vampire like me, I would be able to sense him," I explained.

"I agree that we are not the same. While you were born a vampire, I was made a vampire. Ta make a long story short; I was bitten by a lab rat. Then bad things got worse, good people died, bad people lived, and I guess I did both." There was a touch of remorse in his voice on the last part—a sore spot that seemed to be getting more infected rather than healing.

"If you would allow me to mind link with you, I would like to tell you my story. It is a tale of three boys that endured incredible horrors and bonded together and become brothers of the night. We became the Sons of Darkness." Gerald reached out mentally.

PART 3

Gerald: The Curse and The Cure

1

Lilly walked into the kitchen and came back with a cup of coffee. "You guys may be good, but I need something to keep me coherent," she mumbled as she flopped back on the couch, causing me to bobble a little. Amazingly, she didn't spill a drop.

"When I was little, literally little, I remember hating violence. I mean I liked the movies and all, but actually hitting or even yelling at someone made me sick to my stomach." I leaned back and started telling my horror story.

"I'm tell'n you this now as a warning of the things you may see in the link."

A good starting point of my horror was my last days in a dojo. I sat in the corner of the dojo and I heard Mr. Daleson talking to the judges. Times like this I hated the most, waiting to get in the ring.

Time was painfully dragging on; each second was another eternity. I felt my palms sweating, and the numbness in my chest had slithered down to my forearms. I concentrated on Mr. Daleson's head. I focused on how his receded hairline looked like two afro mountains split between a sea of brass that got wider each day. I thought it was funny how his face looked like he was in his mid-forties, but his body looked like he was in his mid-twenties.

"Who's up next?" asked the short, chubby, chalky skinned guy. I assumed he was our new Safety Observer. He leaned in to scrutinize the remaining students.

One of the assistant instructors replied, "Gerald and Larry. Both are excellent students. Gerald has been coming to class for a while."

Mr. Daleson gave the nod, cueing us to the ring.

"Really, which one is Gerald?" the observer inquired.

"He's the short one there." The assistant instructor pointed me out.

"How old is he?" the observer asked.

"He's sixteen years old." The assistant looked amused.

"You're kidding." The observer chuckles in amusement as he scoped me out.

At the time I was a short kid with what I called a pecan tan. I wouldn't say I was skinny. I referred to myself as wiry and nimble.

"I bet he can't wait till puberty hits. He should add on a couple of pounds if he wants to do well in a competition," the observer continued.

A loud ka-thump echoed through the dojo as I hit the mat.

"See-" (Ka-thump) the observer said, cringing as I hit the mat again.

(Ka-thump)

"Come on, Gerald, you know all the counters; you can do better than this!" Mr. Daleson's deep, scratchy voice beckoned, trying to motivate me to do better.

(Ka-thump)

I saw the observer shake his head and write something on his clipboard.

"Okay, that's enough for today." Mr. Daleson stepped into the ring with a disappointed look on his face. "Let's fall in."

"Bow to me," Mr. Daleson said intensely.

"Respect!" we all yelled out as we bowed to him.

"Bow to the flag."

"Respect," we yelled louder as we bowed to the American flag and the dojo flag.

"Bow to each other."

"Respect!" we all screamed at the top of our lungs.

"Have a good weekend, see you on Monday," blurted Mr. Daleson as the students scurried out the door.

"Gerald, can I have a word with you in the office?"

"Yes sir," I said. I knew what was about to happen. We'd had this conversation before. It had started to be our monthly meeting.

I brushed the sweat from my brow with the back of my hand and wiped it on my pants. As I looked up at Mr. Daleson, I could tell by the wrinkles on his brow that he was upset with me again.

"What happened out there? I watch you practice; you're like a madman on the punching bag. You are beyond expectation with the various weapons we offer. You practice every day, but you don't seem to cut it in the actual sparring match. Are you intimidated by your opponents? If you're scared, say you're scared," said Mr. Daleson in a high-pitched, condescending tone. He was attempting to call out the macho ego that most of the students my age displayed.

"No, I ain't scared! I just don't like fighting and hitting people. I get all numb inside when I hit someone; I hate it. I thought martial arts was supposed to teach you how to control ya self and how NOT to fight. If that's true, den why we gotta go beat up on each other to prove we're good enough to advance?" I asked, though I already knew the answer.

"Look, the name of the game is self-defense. If you don't start showing that you are capable of defending yourself, then there is no

172

reason for you to advance. If you aren't giving it your all, then there isn't any reason for you to be here!"

Mr. Daleson let out a sigh. "Gerald, you're good. When it comes to style and technique, you're maybe one of the best students I have had in a long time; but you need to do some soul-searching this weekend. As much as I like to have you here, you need to decide if here is where you want to be."

With those words, Mr. Daleson walked me to the door. He patted me on the back and gave me one of his rare smiles as I walked out of the dojo.

It was 3:07 p.m. The sun and humidity were at their worst. It was only 90 degrees out. For a spring day in Georgia, it was nice outside.

There was an excessive number of birds singing and flying around. As I walked from the dojo to the car, I had to squint my eyes from the glare of sunlight. It wasn't that dark inside the dojo—was it?

I felt hot, sticky, and drained as I walked to the car. All the leaves on the trees were bright green as if Ted Turner Techni-colored the heck out of them. Even the leaves in the shadow of other trees were brilliant and gorgeous.

My old rusted Toyota Corolla was shimmering as if freshly waxed. Sadly, but funny to say, the rust spots that went clean through the medal in some places were also glistening.

I opened the door and put on my sunglasses. I turned on the engine and cranked up the radio, then pulled out of the parking lot.

"There's a worldwide outbreak of HV2. One out of five people you know may be infected. With your help and donations, we can find a cure and end this horrible plague," the radio announcer requested on the airwaves.

"You bet there will be a cure, and Aunt Helen will find it," I muttered down to the radio as I drove home.

"By 1999 the news passed that the Hyper-Human Immune Deficiency Virus 2 known as HV2, has plagued over fifteen percent of the United States. HV2 has become a global epidemic. From what we know about the Hyper Human Immune Deficiency Virus 2, it destroys the white blood cells and eats away the flesh. The first case of HV2 appeared in 1986; it was thought to be a viral infection that mutated from HIV.

"The biggest problem was the ease with which the virus spread. HV2 could spread through most body fluids; to include blood, sweat, and tears. There are no symptoms of HV2, and there are no blood tests to tell if you or a loved one has contracted the virus. The virus could lay dormant for months or days before the symptoms appeared.

"It is recommended that everyone get a physical done yearly. If you suspect that you or a loved one has encountered someone with HV2, contact your doctor or health care clinic immediately. So, let's take care of ourselves and each other in this mad, crazy world. This has been a public service announcement from Medical Center of Augusta and your hit music station WBUZ, the buzz." The radio announcer came in after the public service announcement and put on an upbeat song to lighten the mood.

5

I looked over to Zarian; he seemed to be getting bored. "Zarian, right? I am not sure if you know this, but Augusta is one of the largest cities in Georgia and is quite popular for its medical centers. Even more so, since the president passed the bill granting support for the research and development to cure the dreadful HV2 disease. Medical centers and hospitals have been jam-packed with people dying from HV2. The entire world seemed to be isolating itself as this disease plagued mankind. Scientists, chemists, and doctors either didn't have a clue of where to begin or stayed away, afraid that they might catch the deadly virus." I leaned back in my seat and continued to drive home.

There were a few that took the challenge and refused to quit. Dr. Helen Jones, a thirty-five-year-old biochemist, was widely known for her breakthrough in her field. Doctors and scientists had watched HV2 grow from a few cases in medical books to a full-scale epidemic.

"I have dedicated my life to finding a cure for this dreaded terror of man," she had been quoted as saying on occasion. She became a beacon of hope in a time where hope was in need. Helen worked day and night diligently, motivated only by her passion for her work and her ambition to be a successful Black woman. At four-feet-eleven inches tall she was a tiny southern belle with a big southern attitude. Anyone opposing her ideas and goals would find that she was a mountain to overcome.

As I pulled into the driveway, I saw Aunt Helen's car. It was the weekend, and I was sure she was busy at work.

"Hello—Aunt Helen, you still down there working?" I yelled down into the basement where she spent most of her time from work—doing more work.

I came to live with my Aunt Helen after my parents died the year before. They were in a car accident—some rich guy—a drunk driver; and the airbags in their car were faulty. It turned out the price for turning my life upside down included a pretty big price tag.

My father had a brother I could have lived with, but Uncle Tony was always between jobs. My social worker figured that my insurance settlement wouldn't last until I finished school because of his debts. I liked Aunt Helen; she let me have my space, and she treated me like an equal. She even gave me a car, sort of.

6

"Yeah," Helen responded. She looked back toward the stairs and watched as I appeared down the stairs.

She worried about me, but she didn't want to let on. She had no experience with children, especially a teenage boy. I wasn't a bad kid; I was just kind of a loner. She thought I had built up anger and trust issues because I refused any assistance in preparing my family's funeral. I didn't mumble a word through the whole terrible ordeal. I just sat quietly and cried with my head down as if I were ashamed of myself. She wasn't sure if I was in shock or if I needed therapy. It had been a year since the death of my parents, and I still did not talk about it.

I warmed up some old pizza and relaxed for a moment. I wasn't too anxious to go down there. I watched a little TV and headed to the basement.

Aunt Helen had converted the basement into a lab after I moved in. She thought it would be a good idea for her to be home more often. In my opinion, it was a wasted effort, because I still didn't see her much. Not that she had no time for me; I just hated to go down there. All the bright lights and machines reminded me of a hospital.

Helen looked at her watch. "It's almost 9:00. So how was kung-fu practice?" Aunt Helen asked with a sarcastic grin, predicting what my reaction would be.

"I told you it's not kung-fu, its karate. There is a difference," I replied as I walked around the cabinets to where she was standing. Her nose was crinkled up with her glasses at the tip. I always thought she looked like a momma bunny rabbit.

"Did you put gas in the-" Helen stopped in mid-sentence to scream. Her face was full of joy and amazement. "Come look, come look!"

"What—what happened?" I said as I rushed over.

Helen pointed at the rat with tears in her eyes.

"You scared me to death, just to see another one of your lab rats," I said in a breathless panic.

Helen's voice cracked with excitement. "Well, yes and no—the rat's name is Meme, He was infected with HV2. He was about to die when I injected him with a new anti-viral drug I created. I think we found it; I think we found a cure."

A unt Helen reached for the phone to call her longtime friend and co-worker Dr. Franklin Wind.

Dr. Frank Wind, also a biochemist, was in his mid-thirties. He was a pale-skinned white man. Not pale as if he were sick, he just did not get to enjoy the sun anymore. His hair was short and neat with salt and pepper around the edges. Frank was tall and lean like a swimmer; most people called him the smart jock. He had worked beside Helen day after day for the past eight years and still found her to be refreshing and innovative as the first day they started working together. They gave each other professional and moral support, maybe more than co-workers usually require. Back then, inter-racial relationships were not very popular in Georgia, so they kept their feelings hidden.

"Hello Kendra, is your father home?" Helen asked.

"Yeah, but he's asleep. Do you know what time it is?" The spite was evident and clear in Kendra's voice.

"Who is it, pumpkin?" Frank asked in the background.

"It's Helen, maybe she called for the time," Kendra smartly remarked.

Kendra and her father had been best friends; they were as close as any father and daughter could ever be. Sometimes she was very defensive, obnoxious, and rude to anyone who would come between her and her daddy.

"Hello, Helen," Frank said, squinting at Kendra, warning her to behave.

"Hi, Frank. Give your daughter hugs and kisses for me."

Frank chuckled. "Funny; I see you're in good spirits."

Helen took a deep breath and let out a sigh of relief "I did it—we did it."

Frank asked in a half asleep, half bewildered voice, "What did you do now?"

"I found the cure," Helen replied.

Frank, now wide awake, blurted out with enthusiasm, "You did it?"

Helen answered back with a high-pitched squeal, "Yes. I'm making the last computer entries as we speak. Come over first thing in the morning, and we'll run another analysis."

"Aunt Helen, I think you better feed your rat; he's eating through the cage," I replied as she hung up the phone.

Aunt Helen rushed over to the cage, grabbed Meme behind the neck, and began to scold him. "Meme, you know better; what's gotten into you?"

"I was wondering, Aunt Helen, since most of the rats look alike; how do you tell them apart?

Helen said, "Well, I know Meme is smaller than the rest of the rats, and they all have computer chips implanted in their backs. That way, if one were to escape, we can track it down from up to ten miles."

I noticed that all the rats in the surrounding cages were at the furthest point from Meme as possible. "Hey, Aunt Helen, why are the other rats scared of Meme?" I asked.

"It is strange, the way the others are acting. Rats have a sixth sense about sick and infected rats; maybe they think Meme is still dying?" Aunt Helen guessed.

I could tell by the way she pushed the glasses up onto her face that she was about to give me a bunch of scientific babble that would put me asleep or in a coma, so I made my move. "Wow look at the time. I have a busy day tomorrow, and I should be heading to bed."

"That's a good idea; we'll talk in the morning. Make sure you lock up before you go to bed," Aunt Helen replied as she looked at her watch. She turned back to her computer and started to finish documenting the miraculous event.

After hours of work, she fell asleep at her computer like she had done many times before. As she slept, Meme chewed through the cage and attacked the other rats, killing all but one.

9

Morning came, and I was heading out to wash the car and run some errands. I yelled upstairs to Aunt Helen's room as I headed out, "Bye, Aunt Helen. I'll be back in an hour so that we can go to the mall and movies."

Down in the basement, Helen heard nothing but the door slamming. Sore and achy from sleeping on the desk, she looked over at the cage and saw the horrible dismembered parts of the lab rats. One rat was lying there on its back, breathing heavily and covered in blood. Helen quickly grabbed him to see which one it was and to find evidence of what happened. Meme suddenly bit Helen on the hand. She screamed in pain, dropping Meme on the floor, where he darted into a corner to hide.

A moment later the door came flying open. Helen looked back to see Frank, and in a flash, Meme was gone.

"What happened? I heard screaming," Frank asked with worry written across his wrinkled brow.

"Frank, it's Meme, he escaped. He bit me and ran off. He's never acted like this before. He chewed through the cage and killed the other lab rats. He played dead and waited for me to pick him up." Helen looked at Frank, a little flustered.

Frank took a look at Helen's hand. "You're bleeding all over the place; we're going to the hospital."

Helen jeered away from him. "No, we have to find Meme before he gets away."

Frank said, "Don't worry about that now; we can find him by his chip—"

The words barely made it out of his mouth when Helen fainted. Frank caught her and carried her up the stairs. Before he could make it out the front door, Helen jumped out of Frank's arms and grabbed him by the neck. She seemed bewildered, confused. The gleam in her eyes indicated anger, and her lips formed a wayward grimace at the sound of Frank gasping for air. She threw Frank to the floor, knocking him unconscious.

Helen flashed back to her senses and realized what she had done. She reached out to help Frank and passed out again. She came to just minutes before Frank, with a hunger that swept across her body, twisting her stomach with pain.

The desire to attend to her injured friend felt unimportant. All she felt was hunger, and Frank smelled good; not like cologne good, more like the essence of life, if bottled as a seasoning or spice. Frank awoke in fear; before a word was spoken, Helen attacked with the fierceness of a savage animal.

Hours later, I returned home. I walked up the driveway and saw Frank's truck.

"If you guys don't stop spending so much time together, people are going to think you're dating." I chuckled as I walked into the house.

I got no response. I walked into the living room and saw the remains of Frank lying on the floor. Helen was crouched over him, licking the blood from Frank's torn flesh.

"Come here, boy," Helen moaned.

Cautiously I approached. I noticed her eyes; they seemed to have a white haze over them like a dead fish in a market. I approached anyway.

Helen grabbed me by the arm, her breath stinky and hot against my skin. The stench of Frank's body churned my stomach. I pulled away and stepped backward.

"Listen to me, boy; I can't fight this much longer. You must find Meme. He's the cause of this; he bit me. The mutation it causes—I can't fight this craving for—" Helen let out a scream of pain and lunged at me.

I countered her attack, softly flipped Helen to the floor, and ran for the front door.

Helen shook it off. "Run, boy," she yelled.

As I looked back, I could see her soul drifting into darkness. I grabbed the keys on the counter and ran out the door. I got in the car and noticed that the keys weren't Helen's or mine. I pushed the lock button and Frank's truck chirped.

"Lucky break, because I ain't going back in that house ever again," I said to myself.

11

As I drove down the street, reality struck me like a bat to the head. I rolled down the window to get fresh air, trying to hold back tears. Today was the second time in my life that I felt all alone. This time, the person I loved wanted to kill me, and I had nowhere to go. The cops would think I was crazy. The only one who could help me was lying dead on our living room floor.

I rode around town for hours trying to collect my thoughts when I saw a light come on in the console. It was the low gas indicator.

"It's time to pull over," I murmured to myself.

A girl came running from across the street "What are you doing in this truck? It doesn't belong to you."

"Do I know you?" I put up a defensive attitude as I started to pump gas. "Who the heck is this?" I asked myself as I gaze up and down her tiny five-foot-five frame.

Her brunette hair rested just at her shoulder. She had a smooth tan like she had laid out on the beach in some exotic island. Her thick eyebrows and rigged nose showed that she was clearly of Italian descent, maybe not full but definitely a part. She dressed like one of those female Mexican gang members, with the dark liner around her lips and extra emphasis on the liner at the corner of her eyes. By the way she walked over here, she sure had an attitude.

The girl responded, "The question should be, do I know you?"

Before I could answer, I was surrounded by a group of guys.

"Is there a problem, Kendra?" a big black guy in a varsity jacket asked.

Kendra replied, "Yes, this dickhead stole my father's truck!"

"Stole? Hey, wait a minute," I protested.

"Shut up, dickhead" another black guy with dreadlocks and a matching jacket demanded.

"Do you know who he is?" a third clean-cut white guy asked.

"No, I've never seen this dickhead before in my life," Kendra stated as her eyes glanced me up and down ready to attack her prey like a lion.

I saw the tension building, so I tried to de-escalate the situation. "Look, I'm not going to be too many more dickheads, so listen to me—"

"**N**o, you listen," the first guy said as he punched me in the face. The other two guys jumped in, and I was overcome with violent blows.

"Now what do you have to say?" the first guy smirked.

Pain swelled through my body, as I let out a faint moan. "I'm Dr. Helen Jones's nephew."

The second guy laughed. "Yeah, buddy, you're going to need a doctor."

Kendra looked down at me with her hand over her mouth. Embarrassment trembled through her voice as she asked, "Are you Helen's kid?"

I nodded before I passed out. The next thing I remembered was waking up in a strange house lying on the sofa with a bag of ice on my head. I sat up, and pain shot across my head. A moan fell from my lips as I looked around for the door to escape.

"Where is my father, dickhead?" a voice from the corner demanded.

"I take it you're Kendra. There is something we need to talk about," I told her as I sat up.

Kendra rose out of the shadows of a corner in the living room. "What's wrong? Is he in the hospital? Where is he? I tried to call, but he's not picking up his cell phone, and your line is busy."

I took a deep breath. It was the first time I had spoken the horror of what took place. My eyes welled with tears. My voice trembled as I told Kendra the news about her father's death.

Kendra jumped out of her seat and started to shake her hands. "My father is dead? You're lying—how could this happen? I thought your mother was supposed to be the best. How could a little rat infect my father and kill him?"

"It's not that simple to explain; we have to go and somehow find that rat before it infects someone else," I tried to explain.

"Are you crazy? I'm not going to go looking for some diseased rat!" she said, folding her arms and glaring at me with her left eyebrow raised.

"I wish I were crazy, but this rat is capable of infecting other people or worse." My eyes drifted down to the hardwood floor. I put my hands over my face; I had a flashback to my parents' funeral. No one should have had to endure something like that twice in a lifetime.

"Well, it seems to me this is a job for the police or something," Kendra stated.

"And what will you tell them? That your father and my aunt found the cure for the plague and tested it on a lab rat that became rabid and bit my aunt and infected her, making her kill your father?"

"Wait a minute. You told me that the rat killed my father; now you say it was your mother?" Kendra said through her teeth. Her body shifted, expressing her defense.

"She's not my mother. She was my aunt."

"Mother, murderer—aunt, no matter; she is going to burn, and so are you. That's why you had my father's truck. How far did you think you would get before I realized he was missing?" Kendra screamed.

As she reached for the phone, I snatched it away. Kendra looked at me with so much hatred and disgust that it took me off guard. I paid for it as she kneed me square between the legs, then delivered a right cross to the jaw that floored me.

"Don't screw with me!" Kendra said as she began to dial the police.

A little surprised and a lot dizzy, I leaned toward the phone and pulled the cord out of the wall.

Totally frustrated now, Kendra slammed the phone on the top of my head. I fell to the floor again; my vision blurred. It felt like the phone was ringing in my brain as I tried to regain my footing.

"You get up again, and the cops won't have anything to haul to jail," Kendra said as she started to run to the back room to get another phone.

As she ran past me, my eyes started to focus, and I grabbed her leg. She fell forward and hit her head on the coffee table.

A stream of blood poured from her head as she lay unconscious on the floor. In a panic, I ran toward the door. I stopped myself. "If I leave and she's hurt, she might die."

14

I came back. "Still breathing—barely," I said, leaning over her. I picked her up as best as I could, straining over her ninety-pound body as I placed her in the truck.

Running every light, I prayed aloud for her to be okay. With a jerk and a few sputters, the truck stopped. I was out of gas. I grabbed her and ran three long blocks, praying for help.

I yelled and screamed for someone, anyone, to help, but no one would help for fear that they might catch the plague from this bleeding young girl.

I reached the hospital lobby. My knees gave way, and I fell to the ground. A lady sitting in the lobby screamed for assistance and two nurses from the counter rushed to our aid. Soon the entire hall was full of people either trying to help or trying to watch. The distraction made it easy for me to sneak out.

I started walking to clear my mind. Time flew by as I walked. I noticed it was almost three in the morning. The dew in the air made my shirt stick to my bruises as I rested on a bus stop bench.

I woke up a few hours later feeling sore, hungry, and alone. The first thing to come to my mind was finding out if Kendra was okay. I pulled out a dime and my last quarter to dial the hospital.

"Hello, I was at the hospital last night when that girl was left in the lobby. I know you can't give me her name; I was just wondering if she was okay," I asked the nurse on call.

"You know, sir, we aren't allowed to give out information about our patients, but since it's been on the news already, I guess it's safe to tell you that she's gone. So, if you want an interview from her, you are too late."

"Gone?" My throat got a hollow lump as I hung up the phone.

"That rat is the cause of this; it's all his fault!" I yelled out, forcing back my tears. "Your time is up; I will find you or die trying!"

I started walking across town, and it seemed to take forever. I tried to hitchhike but getting a ride with dried blood all over me proved impossible. Hours seemed like days as I finally reached my block. When I got closer to the house, I noticed two pizza delivery cars in the driveway.

Not knowing what to expect, I waited patiently for the pizza guys to come outside. After a few minutes had passed, my starvation took over. I decided to sneak a few slices of pizza out of the closest car. Eight slices of pizza later, no one had come out.

I took a deep breath and prepared for the worst as I entered the front door. Cautiously I looked around the place. It was a total mess; the entire house was in shambles.

From upstairs I could hear whispering, moaning, and laughter. I crept up the stairs to find the noise. I came around the corner to see Aunt Helen in bed with two young men; the pizza guys, I suspected. The remains of Frank were at the foot of the bed. As I looked at the two guys, I noticed that their eyes were hazed over like Aunt Helen's. I slipped past Aunt Helen's door and into my room. I grabbed my nunchucks and some extra money from the dresser. I felt my heart pounding in my throat as I tried to slip back past Aunt Helen's bedroom door.

"You were always a noisy child, Gerald," Aunt Helen giggled. "I never thought you would be stupid enough to come back."

The voice from the bed spoke; although words came from Aunt Helen's lips, it didn't sound like the same woman that took me into her home and treated me like a son.

Her voice was scratchy and hollow, spraying out like a loud whisper in my ear.

I pushed the door wide and slowly walked in. I felt my heart sink from my throat to my stomach, and it was churning like crazy.

"Meet my new boy toys, Rob and Jason. Boys, this is my nephew, Gerald. Bring him to me; let's make him a real part of the family."

"This dickhead is your nephew? We met him yesterday at the gas station. You probably don't recognize me without my fist in your eye." Rob chuckled as he walked toward me.

"Yeah, I remember him; he got blood all over my jacket. I owe you," Jason replied as he walked around from his side of the bed.

It would have been easy for me to run, although I probably wouldn't get far. I felt a burning in my head; it was getting hotter the closer they came. I felt as if I were going to faint. My chest felt tight, and it was hard for me to breathe. My hands were sweating; then it dawned on me—it was time to fight. This time was different; this time it was life or death and not a match in the dojo.

Rob reached for my throat; I pushed his hand away and punched him in the throat. Jason came up from behind and grabbed my arms. I did a low back kick that scraped down his shin as I threw my head backward, hitting him in the face. Rob rushed toward me like a locomotive and was floored by a swift right cross from my nunchucks. The fight seemed to go on and on. The bruising from the nunchucks on their skin didn't appear to slow them down. It was as if they no longer felt pain.

I was amazed. I was standing my ground, but for every punch I threw, I realized that they weren't stopping, and I couldn't keep this up forever.

"I've got to find a way to stop these guys—I've got to take this fight elsewhere," I said to myself.

I rushed Jason and scooped him up by the legs, lunging forward, causing him to lose his balance and fall down the stairs.

I slid down the banister and ran to the kitchen. I franticly fumbed through the drawers and found a large knife.

My adrenaline was pumping, and my hands were shaking. I knew that it was either them or me. Would I be able to go through with this? The thought of killing made me sick again, even if it was Rob and Jason.

"You ain't leaving yet, dickhead; I haven't tasted your flesh yet". I'm going to make you die slow," Rob said, creeping through the house looking for his prey.

I took a breath, then stuck my head under the faucet for a drink of water. I could hear the ghoulish jocks getting closer. I ducked behind the kitchen door. The moment Jason walked into view, I stepped out from behind the door and sliced his throat. Jason fell; this time he didn't get up as fast.

"You're going to pay for that," Rob said as he sucker-punched me from behind.

I fell to the floor, dazed. "That was a good one," I mumbled as I cut him across his thigh.

Rob stood there and laughed. "I hope that wasn't your best."

A look of worry crossed my face as I saw Jason begin to rise from the floor. His throat was still cut but no longer bleeding. Rob grabbed me by the shirt and held me in the air. I hit my back on the old china cabinet; I hated that cabinet. My head was throbbing, and every part of my body hurt.

I must have blacked out for a second, because when I looked up, Rob was over me, about to bite me. In a panic, I stabbed Rob in the throat. Rob's eyes were as wide as golf balls as he flinched in pain, stomping my chest into the floor as he flailed away from me.

I stumbled to my feet and fell out the door trying to get to the shed.

It was hot outside even though the sun was going down. I felt the humidity in the air instantly. The heat was causing the bruises, scrapes, and cuts to stink and throb even more.

Even though the shed was only twenty paces away, it felt like it was across town. I finally made it inside and grabbed the machete we bought to trim the Christmas tree last year.

I sensed Jason behind me as he tackled me into the shed. Even though I had just enough time to brace for impact, I landed hard sideways on the lawnmower.

"AHH-" I yelled as the machete fell from my hand and slid behind the tool chest. We wrestled inside the shed, both fighting for possession of the machete, like an old Western movie.

I quickly maneuvered my arm around Jason's neck and twisted until I heard it snap. My mouth dropped to the floor as I watched Jason's neck pop back in place.

Jason stood up and smirked. I swung the machete as hard as I could and chopped Jason's head off completely. I felt my stomach churn; I got dizzy and puked at the sight of Jason's remains. To my relief, I noticed Jason didn't get up this time.

"One down, two to go," I said out loud, trying to build my confidence. "But where is Rob? I'm sure he's up by now."

I felt the sun pressing on my bruises as I pulled the sweat and blood drenched shirt off my body.

I tried to take a deep breath, but all I got was acid reflux. I reached the entryway of the house. My heart pounded in my head with each step I took.

"This is not going to be easy, but this is my house," I muttered under my breath, pumping myself up.

I entered the house from the kitchen, where I last saw Rob. I had hoped to find a trail of blood or something to lead to where he was, but there was nothing there. I continued into the living room. Taking a deep breath, I spotted a dried blood stain on the carpet. I assumed it was from Frank's body. I slowly made my way up the stairs trying to anticipate when Rob would pop out. Every step seemed to creak louder and louder as I made my way to the top.

"GERALD, I know you're there. Come here; boy, I have a surprise for you," Aunt Helen shouted from her bedroom.

As I looked down the hall, each door was closed. The setting sun cast an eerie shadow down the hall. I knew that this was a trap and Rob was nearby, waiting to strike.

I approached Aunt Helen's bedroom door. I felt my palms start to sweat. I gripped the machete tight, took a deep breath, and stepped into Aunt Helen's bedroom. I panned around and found Aunt Helen still lying on the bed. At the foot of the bed, beside Frank's torn and mangled body, was another body—a live body squirming around under the sheets.

"I told you that I had a surprise for you." Aunt Helen's voice was soft, playful, and devious. "Take a look, if you dare."

I walked over to the lump on the floor and pulled the sheets away slowly. I tried to keep an eye on Aunt Helen and whatever was under those sheets at the same time. I felt my breath getting shorter and shorter as I pulled the sheet away.

"Kendra?" I couldn't believe my eyes. I thought she died. She seemed a little shaken, a little scared, and a lot pissed off as she squirmed to get untied.

"Can you believe she came here with a wooden stake to kill me? What do I look like, a movie?" Aunt Helen laughed.

"What do you want from me?" I asked, feeling defeated.

"You know my secret. There's two ways to keep you quiet: I either kill you, or you join me. I would hate to have to kill you, since you are family and all," Aunt Helen stated as she held out her hands, cocking her head to the side, purposely overacting.

"Well, I guess there isn't going to be a family reunion this year," I said, trying to make light of the situation, but the crackle in my voice gave me away.

Out of nowhere, Rob grabbed me from behind so that Helen could attack. I quickly flipped Rob onto the floor and swung the machete, slicing Aunt Helen across the chest just below the neck. Helen fell over the bed and onto the floor. I cut the ropes, freeing Kendra.

Rob got up and screamed at the top of his lungs, "You are dead meat, dickhead."

I jumped up as if I were going to kick Rob in the chest, and at the last second, I kicked him on the kneecap. The blow dropped Rob to the floor. Instantly Rob's knee popped back into place, and he started to get up again.

I let out a karate yell as I jumped into the air, swinging the machete down on Rob's head. As three-quarters of Rob's head rolled under the bed, I noticed I wasn't as sick as before.

"Kendra, run!" I yelled as I waited for Aunt Helen to arise from behind the bed, but there was no sound.

Cautiously I made my way to the other side, where Helen fell. As I approached the far side of the bed, Helen reached from under the bed and pulled me to the floor. I let out a startled yell as my head bounced off the hardwood floor.

I kicked and yelled like a zebra captured by a lion. All that kicking must have knocked the support beams under the bed loose because the bed came crashing down as I squeezed from under the box spring and boards, and I saw Aunt Helen struggling out after me.

I fumbled around on the floor trying to find that darn machete. As my fingers ran down the body of the blade and onto the handle, my eye began to burn. I reached back and struck as her head appeared from under the heap. The blade went through her neck and stuck in a board on the floor.

As I walked out of the bedroom, I puked on the floor so hard it felt like my insides were trying to come out of my throat. I walked downstairs and look around. Everything was dark and gloomy, like there was a big storm brewing in my head.

In the kitchen, Kendra's eyes were focused on something out the window, out toward the shed. She watched the remains of Jason's body slowly melting. I passed by, barely noticing her as I saw the horrible sight of someone melting in the yard.

"Yo dude, do they all go out like that?" Kendra asked with amazement.

"I don't know!" I replied. "I've never killed anyone! Hell, maybe all people die this way. How do I explain this to the cops? I'm going to be in jail or a mental institution for the rest of my life."

"Well, how many more are there like them?" Kendra asked.

"I don't know; this all started when Meme bit Aunt Helen. Oh, my damn! If Meme bites someone else, then this whole thing will start over! I have to find that rat!" I blurted out as my tunnel vision locked in on my only purpose in life.

"Did you just say, 'Oh my damn'? Never mind. How are you going to find one rat in the city? I mean, you can find rats anywhere, but how are you going to find that particular one?" Kendra asked

"Aunt Helen said something about each lab rat having a computer chip that can pick up a signal from up to ten miles."

I turned on the water faucet and stuck my head in. The cold water felt soothing on my bruised and bloody face. I took a big gulp of water and leaned back to brush the remaining blood, sweat, and water from my face. I gritted my teeth as I wiped my swollen palms and cut knuckles on my jeans.

"Let's look downstairs. Maybe we can find a way to find Meme." I looked over at Kendra, and for the first time I noticed her eyes; they were as blue as the sky and so peaceful, and for that brief moment, I thought of the song "Modern Love" by David Bowie—why, I don't know, but for that brief instant, all of my aches and pains disappeared.

"Gerald, you seem different from the other day. You were kind of wimpy before. I thought to myself, 'I'm gonna die for sure' when I heard it was you who was there to rescue me. I mean, the way you stood up to Rob was pretty good for a small guy like you," Kendra said in her most sincere manner.

"Thanks, I think-." Confusion was posted all over my face as I turned on the downstairs light.

"So, what does this thing look like?" Kendra asked as she quietly marched down the stairs behind me.

"I have no idea; I was hoping one of these boxes will say tracer or tracker or something. If not, we are going to have to open each one of them."

After what seemed like a lifetime, Kendra spoke from across the room. "I think I found it."

"Let's see what you got," I said with an exhausted demeanor.

"So, now that we have the mouse trap; let's go catch a mouse," Kendra commented.

Even the vengeful look on her face looks cute, I thought to myself.

I grabbed the keys to Aunt Helen's car on the way out. That song popped into my head again. I started to chuckle inside. "This must be our theme song," I said under my breath.

"The sun is going down; I hate this time of day," Kendra stated. "It's not dark, it's not light, but it is very annoying."

We got to Helen's car, a Ford Mustang, Aunt Helen's only spot of vanity.

"Can you drive a stick?" I looked over to her.

"NO!" Kendra answered, looking at me, waiting for me to say something chauvinistic.

"Well then, I'll drive, and you try to work that thing." I chirped the car, unlocking it, then flopped into the driver's seat.

Kendra flipped a switch and started the machine. Whistles, beeps, and bright flashes filled the car. Turning some knobs and pushing buttons, Kendra finally got the machine under control. The tracker thing started pinging signals from the house and another single ping a few blocks away. Just like that, we began our journey.

Doubt filled my mind as we drove block after block trying to find that stupid rat. I asked myself, *what am I going to do? What is she doing?*

I looked over at Kendra, who was trying to figure the direction of the blip on the screen as we coasted down the road. "Why are you helping me? I thought you were going to the police?"

"To be honest with you, I did go to the police, and they laughed at me and said I was imagining everything because of my concussion. So, I went to your aunt's house to kill her myself," Kendra said bluntly

"I appreciate your honesty; I am glad that through all of this we turned out to be friends."

Kendra turned to me with a straight face. "Friends, who said we are friends? I don't make friends with dickheads."

I look over at her, not sure if she was joking or not. I sighed in relief as I notice her smile.

"Relax; it's us against the world." Kendra giggled and gave me a sock on the arm. I winced a little and gave a macho chuckle, not wanting her to know that it really hurt.

Going through all the events in my head, something dawned on me. "There was one left!" I said out loud as I stop the car and turn around.

"What are you talking about?" Kendra asked

"There was another rat that was experimented on; for some reason it didn't run from Meme, and Meme didn't kill it like it did the others. If so, then we could use it against Meme," I told Kendra as we headed back to the house.

At the driveway, Kendra looked at me. "Are you ready?"

I stepped out of the car and sighed. "I've done this twice already, and each time there was something worse inside. I don't know if I can ever be ready for this, but let's go anyway."

Cautiously we walked inside. We looked around and didn't see anything different. We made our way down the stairs to the lab. I looked on the counters as Kendra looked through the computer.

"I found a file on the different treatments that your aunt was giving the lab rats. She actually kept good records for someone who couldn't keep up with the times of day. How do we know which rat is the one you are looking for?" Kendra asked.

"That is the easy part; it is the rat that looks the buffest. Here it is—number fifteen," I said as I spotted the caged lab rat still in its cage.

The cage had been tossed on the ground but was still intact. The muscles on the rat were huge, but the rat was content in its cage and didn't try to escape.

Kendra punched the number fifteen on the computer.

"The rat's name is Lou. He was injected with some sort of red blood cell steroid derivative. If we inject ourselves, maybe Meme won't attack us. Your aunt even wrote out the formula for humans according to weight. The vials are supposed to be in the refrigerator," Kendra said, reading Aunt Helen's notes.

"For one, neither of us is a doctor, and we aren't going to experiment on each other." I blurted words of caution.

"Well, at least let's take it with us just in case," Kendra pushed the issue.

I agreed, and we began to calculate our weight for what we could only assume was a repellant or cure from whatever is out there. I put number fifteen's cage back on the counter. If we failed and someone came across this, maybe our deaths wouldn't be in vain.

We got back in the car and restarted out adventure. As we drove down the road, Kendra got a signal on the tracker.

"Turn left here—that rat is just up ahead," she directed.

"It figures. Meme is heading toward the high school. It's bad enough I have to go to school all day, now I'm here at night," I commented.

"It gets worse; there is a baseball game tonight. It's five o'clock, and both teams should be in the locker rooms by now. If that rat gets in there, there's definitely going to be trouble," Kendra pointed out.

You know rats usually stay away from large crowds of people? This one was heading toward them.

"It's as if Meme wants to infect people," I said.

"That's crazy; rats aren't that smart—are they?" The look on Kendra's face showed the fear that I was trying to suppress.

"Calm down! Rats are pack animals; I think since it has always associated with people Meme may think that people are its pack. But we can't worry about that now. We have to get Meme before it infects anyone else. Besides, our team sucks so there won't be that many people at the game," I told Kendra, trying to convince her . . . and myself.

As we made our way into the school parking lot, the signal beeped more repetitiously. I parked the car around the corner down from the school.

"Why are you stopping here?" Kendra asked

"Well, just in case we have to make a run for it, we can split up and meet back here and regroup, or haul ass."

"That's fine, but if you leave me, I will kick your ass, and you know I can," Kendra warned.

W e slowly made our way through the school, moving closer to the beeps. I started to feel a familiar sense of dread as we walked down the corridors past each empty classroom.

Unknowingly I started singing under my breath "Never going to fall for—"

"Modern love," Kendra added.

"Once beside me."

"Modern love," she said, looking over at me

"Walks on by—"

"Modern Love." She smiled, and her blue eyes magically pierced my heart.

"Gets me to the church on time," we sang together, and for that moment we made a connection that seemed to last for hours.

My gaze into her magical blue eyes was quickly broken by the loud tone of the tracker. Back to reality.

"At least it's away from the baseball field and the gym," Kendra said with a sigh of relief.

As we reached the end of the corridor, there was a single tone from the tracker.

"It must be in here," Kendra replied

"Stay behind me," I said defensively.

"What—is that some kind of macho male chauvinist comment?" Kendra whispered with resentment.

"No, but I'm the one with the machete," I responded, holding up our only weapon.

Kendra paused for a minute, then took a step back.

I opened the door quickly but carefully. Cautiously, we stepped inside the door. The lights came on, and several people were standing in the back of the classroom.

"The Master told us you were coming; it didn't take you too long," said a voice in the crowd.

"I think they are just in a hurry to die," said another.

As I looked across the room, I counted the people. Three teachers, three students, and what seemed to be a janitor or maintenance man; all of their eyes were hazed over like Aunt Helen's.

I got even more worried when I heard Kendra breathing heavily behind me. I thought I could take two or three out, four if I got lucky. But what about Kendra? I knew I could handle myself, but how well could she defend herself? Now wasn't the time to find out.

I whispered as softly as possible. "Kendra, back out slowly into the hall and—"

Without fear, Kendra ran past me and attacked the ghouls, screaming with hatred, like a warrior in battle. She gave a swift kick to one of the student's heads, sending him to the floor. She moved toward the rest of the group with no hesitation.

I joined in, amazed at how Kendra was kicking butt. I refused to be outdone, as I started to fight. I withdrew into my world. My only thought was not to let these monsters out of this room. They all must be destroyed. The screams of the ghouls got louder as the battle escalated.

Suddenly, I heard a different kind of scream. I turned around and saw Kendra being ripped apart by three of the ghouls. I rushed to her aid, then the light went out. I kicked over chairs, frantically trying to reach her, and then there was silence. I stopped to listen; I slowly turned, trying to feel the dark room with my ears. The lights came back on, and everyone was gone.

I ran into the corridor and found a trail of blood. In a panic, I ran after it, out of the school and into the parking lot. I was gasping for breath and hope. The trail of blood ended at my feet. Tears built up in my eyes as I stepped over her legs and walked toward the rest of her body.

"Doesn't that just tear you apart?" A voice laughed behind a car.

"I am going to make you regret being born," I yelled into the darkness.

I ran toward the dark voice; then I felt something bite me on the ankle. I looked down and saw Meme.

"NO!" I yelled out.

I reached into my pocket for what I hoped was the cure, but it was gone. I started to panic. I felt my body begin to change.

I fell to the floor, and my body started convulsing. I looked across the ground and saw a syringe, but it wasn't mine—it was Kendra's. I thrust the needle into my leg and passed out.

When I awoke, I was in the gym. Two hours had passed, and I noticed I was surrounded by dead bodies and a multitude of ghouls.

"I saved you some flesh, just in case you woke up hungry," a voice said to me. But I didn't hear it with my ears—it was more like I heard it in my mind.

It was Meme; the drug must have increased his intelligence as well as giving him the ability to communicate telepathically.

"You must be starving about now. You know, you are very resourceful. That is why I spared you. I need someone to help lead my dominion so that my kingdom will grow as I create new servants."

"I would rather die than serve a rat," I said as I reached out to grab Meme.

I was attacked from behind by one of the ghouls. I turned around to counter his attack. I felt stronger as I fought—so strong that I ripped the head off of the ghoul with my bare hands, like popping the top off a beer bottle.

Meme tried to scurry to safety, but I quickly snatched him up.

Meme started squealing and hissing, but to no avail, as I twisted his neck away from his body. Upon seeing this, the remaining ghouls scattered from the gym. I caught a few and put them out of their misery. Regrettably, some got away, and there was no way to track them.

Unlike Aunt Helen, these things didn't seem to be able to speak or think. That was the good news. The bad news was that they were still ruthless killers.

I got to the car and brought it around to Kendra. I picked her up and placed her in the back seat. Then I took off my torn, blood-stained shirt and put it on top of her.

I drove to the only place I considered home. I pulled the car around back and dug a grave. I sat there in the dark of the night, mumbled a small prayer, and laid her to rest.

It was almost two o'clock in the morning. I rested for a minute on the back porch. My body was weak and bruised; my mind was numb with exhaustion. I went into the house to get a change of clothes. As I journeyed up the stairs, I refused to look in Helen's room. The lump in my throat got bigger as I walked past her doorway. I grabbed a few items of clothes, stuffing them in an old duffel bag.

"Whoa," I said as I got sick to my stomach, sharp pains shooting through my body.

I stumbled to the bathroom and got a sip of water from the sink. I looked in the mirror and noticed my face. My skin was clammy and dark, my eyes were as black as coal, and my fingernails were long and sharp.

"Meme's bite must have had a different effect on me," I said to myself.

"I've got to get out of here," I said in a panic, not knowing exactly where I was going. I grabbed my bag and hopped in my car.

Exhausted, I drove to the nearest hotel. I paid for the hotel room with the MasterCard Aunt Helen got me to build my credit.

"It's to teach you responsibility. So, use it for emergencies only," Helen had said.

I remember telling her, "If I am responsible, then there won't be an emergency." We both laughed. I was going to miss her laugh.

The clerk didn't ask for an ID; she just looked at me very nervously and gave me a key. Stumbling into the room, I lay on the bed for a few minutes. I decided to take a bath to soothe my aches and pains. As I ran water in the tub to take a long hot bath, I noticed that there were no towels in the bathroom. I called for the maid to bring some up. After about twenty minutes, the maid brought towels to the door. My body ached almost unbearably as I sluggishly made my way to the door.

When I opened the door to get the towel, I recognized the maid; she was a student in my karate class. She said hi and hugged me. At the moment I squeezed her close to me, her body fell limp. I realized that it was because of me, and I let her go. I quickly brought her inside and put her on the bed. I went to the bathroom and wetted one of the towels she brought.

Whatever just happened revived me, and I felt good; not one hundred percent, but refreshed. As I ran the water in the sink, I glanced in the mirror and hardly recognized the person looking back at me.

My skin was fresh and clear—not even a zit in sight. My eyes were brown again, but lighter than before. I have grown at least a foot taller.

Whoa, my arms—I was buff. "Taking Kendra's serum after the bite must have made me a super ghoul, but they feed on flesh and blood, and I just drained her energy by touching her," I said, speaking out loud.

I picked up the maid and set a pillow under her head. I checked her pulse to see if she was alright. She seemed fine, but I hated to leave her like that. I thought it would be best to move on. I repacked my bag and went without saying a word. Getting another hotel was too expensive, so I drove to an abandoned warehouse and crashed for the night.

"Morning already? Oh man, I feel bad. Is this what a hangover feels like? I ache all over, almost as bad as before."

I looked at my watch. "It's five o'clock in the evening! I slept here all day, and no one came by. I guess with the spread of HV, no one wants to get involved."

I felt hunger start to brew in my stomach, and my mild headache grew bigger.

I knew it wasn't food that I was craving. I refused to attack an innocent person even if it meant that I would starve to death. "Before I go, I will take down as many of those damn monsters as I can!"

First, I needed some new clothes. I couldn't believe I wore such bright colors.

"If I'm going to hunt the rest of those ghouls, then I have to find more stealthy clothes," I said out loud.

I glanced across the street and saw a thrift store. I went in and picked out a few black rayon shirts, a few more black cotton shirts, four pairs of black denim jeans, and two long black trench coats. I grabbed an old police scanner on my way to the cash register. As I placed the stuff on the counter, I rested my eyes on two butterfly swords displayed in the glass case under the cash register.

"I'll take those too," I told the clerk.

"Pretend'n ta be a ninja or something?" the clerk asked humorously. She was a middle-aged black lady with a platinum-blonde wig. The wig seemed to match her down-south attitude.

I looked up at her with a blank stare. It was the same kind of sarcasm my Aunt Helen used to have.

"Sorry, sir, I was jus' pull'n yo leg. I don't mean noth'n by it," the clerk said apologetically.

"No, don't ever apologize for who you are; my mind was somewhere else," I replied as I paid for my items and left.

I put the clothes in my car and drove back down the street to the warehouse. I washed off with the rainwater in an old barrel and got dressed.

"It's time to go hunting," I said out loud, for self-motivation.

I walked back toward my car. I saw two guys trying to break in.

"Can I help you?" I yelled out.

"Yeah, you can give me your money and the keys," said one of the carjackers.

"You want it, come and get it, but I promise it won't be fun," I told them. I tried to sound like I was in a Clint Eastwood movie.

My eyes turned pitch black, my fingernails formed into small claws, and my teeth grew into small fangs.

Freaked out at the sight of me, one of the carjackers pulled a gun. I was at least twenty feet away; in a flash, I was on top of him. Knocking him out with one punch, I even surprised myself.

The other guy tried to run, but I was way too fast. I bit him on the neck, while he screamed for his life. I had mercy on the thief and didn't kill him.

The thief looked up at me, half conscious. "You should have killed me; it would have been better than dying from HV." Then he passed out.

I stood up and walk over to the other thief. I was dismayed; the hunger I felt was worse. I started to get weak and dizzy as I approached the thief.

"Why don't I feel better? I thought all ghouls ate flesh," I said out loud. I was starting to talk to myself aloud a lot lately. "If you want to live, take your friend and leave right now." I grabbed the thief by the throat to show how dangerous I was.

As I picked the thief up in the air, I got a surge of power. I watched as the thief's body fell limp.

"Oohhh, that's how this works—with a simple touch, I can feed. That means I don't have to bite or kill anyone," I said with a sigh of relief. Then I let the thief's limp body flop to the ground.

32

I got in the car and drove off. I had no plan for where to go. I had no idea of how to find the rest of the ghouls, or even how many were made by Meme.

It was a little after nine o'clock at night. I decided to pull over and take a rest from driving. Needing to stretch my legs, I took a walk down an alley to take a leak behind a dumpster.

Suddenly I felt a burning sensation on the back of my right hand. As I walked further down the alley, my hand tingled more and more. I looked at the ground and saw a trail of blood.

"That smell—I can smell death in the air," I said out loud. Cautiously, I walked down the alley; my body instantly changed to that demonlike form again. This time I felt it and was aware of the change.

Out of the blue, a ghoul jumped out from behind a dumpster.

"Hey, brother—don't be shy. There is plenty for all. I almost didn't sense you. You must be very weak." The ghoul spoke in a low, raspy tone.

"Wrong answer. I'm not your brother, and I'm not weak, either." I growled the words as I made my approach.

"I know you; you're the one who killed the master. But I won't be that easy. The longer we live and feed, the more powerful we become. You may have been able to beat me before, but you have no chance now," the ghoul said. Reaching down, he picked up the dumpster and threw it at me.

I did a back flip—well, more like a side flip backward at an angle. I was a little short on the rotation, so I kind of fumbled to a crouch position. I quickly pulled one of the butterfly knives from the sheath on my side. I tried to make it one fluid motion to seem like the move was on purpose. In a flash, the ghoul was face to face with me. He grabbed my hand and throat, pressed me against the alley wall, and tried to bite me.

"You're right. The longer you live, the stronger you become. It's time for you to die," I grunted as I pulled the other sword out from under my coat and beheaded the ghoul.

I slowly faded back to looking human as I headed back to my car. "I need to learn how to control this change, or it is going to get more dangerous for me," I muttered, trying not to speak out loud to myself.

"Now I know I have to find them all. Soon the ghouls will be too strong for me to destroy," I continued.

I got a room at the cheapest hotel I could afford and kicked back. I watched the news, hoping to find out if they found Frank's body at the house, or at least a suspicious clue to find a ghoul.

After the commercial something incredible came on, it was breaking news. It seemed that the cure for the dreaded plague HV2 had been found. A man with the HV2 had been treated for a bite on the neck at the local hospital.

He said some wild man attacked him and bit him for no reason. It turned out that the saliva from my bite, mixed with the infected victim, had a strange effect on the HV2 virus. The victim had been cured of the virus. A sample of the victim's blood was taken in the hopes of making a vaccine.

With a push from the FCC, the vaccine could be ready within the next year. Cheers were heard in the anchor room as the newscaster made the report.

"Well, Aunt Helen, you did it—your life's work to find the cure is a reality at last. I wish you were around to see it," I said with a lump in my throat. I closed my eyes to keep back the tears and slowly drifted asleep.

PART 4

Czun Eljeye: The Wolf in Man's Clothing

Then there is Czun, the youngest of all. He was the least human of us. Sometimes, Grey, our other brother, would call him a human, to get under his skin.

"I see you look confused, Lilly. Let me explain it to you as he had explained it to me… over and over again. For tho', sometimes he acts like a broken record!" I settled back and started Czun's story.

"Throughout history, in almost every culture, there were stories of men and women that weren't quite human. The minotaur, centaurs, mermaids, and even angels (men and women with bird-like wings) were some of the popular myths. The Sphinx, along with other hieroglyphic drawings on the walls of pyramids, displayed numerous men and beasts combined into one. Often when a man loses control of himself or gets angry, they say he is like a raging beast. This story is not a story of a boy with the spirit of a beast. It is about a beast that lives his life alongside man."

The evolution of man had always caused an ecological imbalance, either for man or for nature. In this particular case, a man named Ohan Mandi was building a new civilization in the midst of a jungle. Mandi found his fortune in a foreign land. He felt he should repay his community by building houses for his people, while making a small profit.

The more he built, the more jungle was destroyed, and the animals retaliated. Mercenaries and hunters were sent in to clear out the potential dangers. To animal lovers, this was an outrage. The sky-high trees and thick foliage that once were home for hundreds of species of wild creatures were being torn down. There was nowhere for the animals to go, so they would venture into the towns and villages of man. The animals' intrusion caused a conflict for man, and that was why they were being destroyed.

The jungle was the birthplace and home of everything untamed and wild. Sometimes the animals that lived in the jungle wore clothes and walked on two legs. These animals lived in cities, but for some reason or another returned to the jungle for money, sport, refuge, or a combination of the three.

To make things interesting, Mandi decided to put prices on different types of animal carcasses to resell for a higher value. The rarer the animal, the more valuable the hide.

It was late in the evening, the sun was going down, but the air was still humid. Most of the men had been in the jungle all day. They came back to the compound smelling and looking as if they just fought a war, and some may have. At the compound, there were trading posts that let men buy and sell supplies needed for survival in these dangerous surroundings. The trading post was the center of the campground—a place where the hunters relaxed, drank, and told the stories of their latest adventure.

Most of the hunters here were refugees from other countries. Some were criminals escaping their fate, and some only crawled from under their rocks to step on others.

Two of the most dangerous hunters in the camp were Mark and Tim. They hung together as if they were brothers but were equally menacing apart.

Mark looked across the table with disgust. "Here comes Xavier. That's the third lion this week."

Tim said, "Yeah, kind of funny how he didn't use traps and he never bought ammo."

"Well, whatever he used blasted the guts right out of the animal, almost ruining the pelt," Mark sneered.

"All I can say is his method may be crude but the money he loses on the quality of carcass he makes up in quantity," Tim remarked, wiping off sweat and camouflage paint from his face.

"I say we do a little recon tomorrow to find out what's going on," Mark replied with a look of mischief that most kids got when they were sure they wouldn't get caught with their hands in the cookie jar.

Tim said, "And if we don't find anything, we can get rid of the competition. All kinds of things could happen to a man out in the jungles."

The sun has barely started to rise. Morning had come too early for Xavier Eljeye as he slumped out of his tent. At first glance, it was apparent he was out of place. He was about 5'9", he had a well-kept trimmed beard, manicured nails, and looked as if the only manual labor he had ever conducted was lifting food to his mouth. Xavier had a dark tan and belly bulge that made him look like Santa Claus on vacation.

The other hunters on the compound had left hours ago.

Xavier seemed to intentionally wait until all the hunters and poachers were long gone.

He stretched his arms and took a breath of the sweet smell of clean morning air. A smile crossed his face as a morning mist brushed over his body. He finished dressing as Wanii, Abo, and Scar—his local guides and hunting crew members—entered his tent.

"Are you ready to go, boss?" asked Scar, his top tracker.

The name Scar was given to him because of the crescent-moon-shaped birthmark on his right cheek. He also had a scar that stretched across his forehead, around the right side of his head, down the back of his neck, and continued down the right side of his back.

Scar and Wanii had been best friends since birth. They both learned the harsh wages of the war when they were children when a rival village attacked theirs. They both became poachers to earn money to buy guns and food to provide for their village.

Scar held a deep hatred for other villages. His mother had been beaten to death in an attack when he was younger. He tried to stop them, but he was too small. One of the attackers grabbed him and threw him to the floor so hard he broke his collarbone. But that wasn't enough; the attacker began to carve on the little boy as if he were going to skin him alive. Then there was a gunshot. It was Leon, Scar's father, who had gone hunting with Wanii's father, Ali. Leon managed to fire two rounds, killing two attackers before receiving a fatal shot.

In all the commotion, Wanii slipped in through the back and grabbed Scar, dragging his friend into the jungle to safety. Since then the two had been almost inseparable.

Xavier smiled. "Let's go get my cage, and we can begin."

238

It seemed like yesterday when Xavier began hunting for pay. In reality, it had been many years since he had been out of the bush. The reason why Xavier ended up in the jungle was unknown. Some say that he was a college professor who got tangled up in a crime ring. Xavier only talked about his home and his past once or twice in a drunken stupor, and he was barely understandable then. The college professor rumor would explain how he was so good at teaching the locals how to speak English with such passion and understanding. No one had ever asked; sometimes people came to the jungle for reasons best left unknown.

Today started like any other. Wanii and Scar headed out in front looking for tracks of any game that would bring in big money. Abo was far less skilled than Wanii and Scar. His job was to guard Xavier—or more appropriately, be a go-between in case of an attack. Some called him "adobo," a raw food dipped in spice. He was there to prevent Xavier from being eaten or raided. If he could kill the predator, great; if not, he was to throw himself in front of the danger, to be shot or eaten. Either way, he was paid well, and in the event of his death, his family would be well compensated.

Several miles into the jungle, they heard a rustle in the brush up ahead. Xavier and Scar aimed and set to shoot when a baby rhino stumbled out. The men all laughed as the baby scurried off in fright. Then in the clearing to the left of the group, a roar blared out—all the men scattered for their lives. A pissed momma rhino was on a rampage to protect her young. As the rhino stampeded through the men, it knocked over the covered cage. Out came a strange beast about 3 feet tall, but it roared like it was 20 feet high.

The rhino turned to the beast and charged. The beast stood its ground, with its fur-covered body spiked up defensively. It flashed large teeth and sharp claws. A millisecond from the point of the rhino's impact, the beast dodged and attacked, slicing down the side of the rhino; like a steak knife cutting cheese. The rhino backed away quickly and prepared to make another pass at the little beast. Then a gunshot echoed through the air; the rhino fell dead. Xavier blew a whistle, and the beast scurried back into the damaged cage.

From behind the trees, the two spying hunters popped up, surprised that a little creature like that could stand up to a massive beast like a rhino

Mark said, "What the hell is that thing?"

Tim said, "I bet that's how he killed all those animals without traps and ammo."

Mark said, "I wish we had found out sooner; then we wouldn't be working so hard to make a living out here." He pulled a handkerchief from his pocket to wipe his brow.

Tim said, "If we take that thing with us, we won't ever have to work again."

Mark and Tim stepped into the clearing. Wanii and Scar were processing the large rhino for sale. Wanii spotted the two men out the corner of his eye. Wanii tried to sneak over to his gun but was shot by Mark. Scar, in a rage, pulled his knife and threw it at Mark, stabbing him in the shoulder. Tim shot Scar in return and pointed his rifle at Xavier.

Tim said, "Now teach me how you trained that thing, or you will die a hell of a lot slower than they did."

Xavier replied, "It has nothing to do with training; it's a smart creature."

Mark stood up, pulling the large knife from his left shoulder, inches away from his heart. "Just kill him, and let's get out of here. I need to get this looked at before I bleed to death."

Tim took aim between Xavier's eyes when something miraculous happened—the beast spoke.

"No, stop!" a childlike voice yelled from the cage where the beast had taken cover. As the men looked over, they saw what looked like a cross between the beast that attacked the rhino and a human child.

Tim looked at the creature and then looked back at Xavier. "What the hell is that thing? Did you do something kinky with one of these animals out here?"

Xavier looked over at the beast with amazement. "You can talk? Why haven't you ever talked before?"

Czun said, "I afraid you hurt me, I scared."

"This is even better! We will make millions with this thing," said Tim, running his hands through his hair.

"Just get him back in the cage. I'm dying here!" Mark grunted in pain.

"Okay, okay; let me just finish Xavier off," Tim demanded.

"No!" Czun roared, and with incredible speed leaped forward, slashing off Tim's arms and biting through his jugular.

Mark was clawed across the neck and on a snap, he was dead.

Xavier, unsure of the intentions of the beast, who now talked, ran in fear. But he was not fast enough, and soon he was tackled to the ground by the beast.

"Why you run. I no hurt?" Czun's little voice muttered.

Xavier looked up in fear. He didn't see the beast; instead, a little boy about ten years of age stood above him.

"You look human—how can this be possible?" asked Xavier

"You found me. I afraid. Humans bad. Xavier good sometimes. Bad men bad all time. I stay with Xavier. No go with bad men. I look like human. Xavier friend now?" Czun tried to explain. He was getting a grasp of the English language, but he was not sure if he was getting his point across.

8

"What are you? Where are you from?" asked Xavier.

"I were-person. We live on island. Very far. One-time man and animal lived together. We had peace. We animals wanted to be like man. We began to stand up. We began to talk your language. Over time we changed. We lost our—fur—" Czun paused, looking for the correct word.

"Man feared us. Tried to divide us. They made—killing tool? Weapons," Czun corrected himself.

"Man would not teach us to use tool-weapons. We became afraid. We became angry. Man-made us war. We no fight. We fled." Czun took a breath to think about his next words and then continued.

"We got on our rafts, and the Ocean-Were help us get away. The Flying-Were found land far away. We went to island. Our new home away, Were Island."

"I can see why you were afraid of us. We made you leave your home," Xavier said with sympathy.

"Don't be sad. I not born yet. I not see old home." Czun tried to smile, but it didn't look quite right.

"Not you type man. Older—um ancient man? Thousands of time ago man. Man changed a lot; we change a lot. We look like man but can look like animal. I am not good at all animal. I look like all animal; my head gets dark. I feel anger in my heart. I can't stop anger."

"If you made it to the island, why did you get on the raft I found you on?" Xavier was wide-eyed at the tale being told by what he referred to in his mind as an animal boy.

"Our people lived on Were-Island for thousands of years. We saw man over time. Planes, not planes, big boats sometimes passed by. The trash would wash up on land. Sometimes the Ocean-Were would find things in the water. We would search them, learn from them. Sometimes man would get lost and find us. They stayed. They died, either injured or old age. We no kill.

"One day the big hill got hot. The air got black. It made hot rocks come down. It bled hot rocks. The ground shook. We ran to the edge of island to get help from the Ocean-Were. They were screaming, the water was bubbling. The Flying-Were fell from the sky. There was no place to hide. My father grabbed me and my mother. He pushed us on a raft. We floated away. We were in the boat long time. Father caught no fish, Mother slept a lot and one day didn't wake. Father gave me the last of water, then he slept and didn't wake. We finally drifted here. I was really weak and sleepy when you came and helped me," Czun explained.

9

"So, you're telling me that you can turn into that beast any time you want?" asked Xavier.

"No, I not human. I Were-Person, a wolf, I change to look human," Czun explained to Xavier

"Do you have a name?" asks Xavier

"Yes, I Czun."

"How did you learn to speak English?" asked Xavier.

"I listen. You teaching the people at night."

Overwhelmed by the events that just happened, Xavier thought it was time to leave the jungles and go back to the states. He contemplated for a moment. "Where is Abo?"

"Him, that way. He run away. Him fast man." Czun let out a snort.

"Figures!" Xavier stomped his foot. "Anyhow, I know you can handle yourself out here in the jungle alone, but if you want you can come with me, back to the States. There are some conditions; you must do everything I tell you and follow my rules. Rule number one; no one must know you are a beast, werewolf, or whatever. Rule number two; no more killing—that goes for animals and man. And rule number three; you must never tell anyone about today or where you are really from. What do you think? Can you handle that?" asked Xavier.

"I will do as you say," Czun replied.

Later that night, Xavier snuck into the village. packed his things. and left. They flagged down a safari tour the next morning, then hitched a ride to a landing strip.

After a week of dodging around airport security and customs, Xavier and Czun finally reached California.

It took some underground dealing, but Xavier finally got Czun a fake birth certificate and even adoption papers. They spent days shopping for clothes. At night, Xavier taught Czun about table manners, etiquette, and ways he could blend in with humans better.

Xavier was known to be a world traveler, so, when an older white man appeared out of nowhere with a kid, it looked suspicious. Czun had a caramel complexion with strong African structured cheekbones and thick loose curls. Some assumed Xavier had a fling with a local, got her pregnant, and brought the child back with him. Czun could easily pass for a biracial child.

It had been five years since they were in the jungle. Czun was a teen-ager now. With some practice, he had learned to manipulate his appearance better. He looked like a regular boy with a few exceptions. For some reason no matter how hard he tried, he couldn't keep his ears from pointing at the top, and his eyes were a yellowish-brown color resembling a wolf.

"I guess these are the things I just can't control." He would say to himself.

Czun's hair was brown and very curly. He wore it short on top and on the sides with long curly dreads in the back; he called it his trademark.

Both black and white humans seemed to treat him different, He didn't quite fit the social mold of either group. His real friends didn't care, because they thought of him as a good friend that made every day an adventure in life.

Xavier and Czun had learned a lot about each other in the time that they traveled together, and they became close friends.

People thought they were father and son, and eventually, they were like father and son. After what seemed to be an eternity of moving from city to city, they ended up in a small two-bedroom apartment near the beach in San Diego, California.

One day, Czun came home from school and found the house all packed up and Xavier ready to get on the move.

"What's going on here?" Czun asked.

"Well, remember that the money I said I borrowed a while back? The guy I borrowed it from, found out where we are and now, we have to leave, tonight," said Xavier.

"But I don't want to go! I wanted to finish school here, I want to go to college here!" Czun yelled, slinging his backpack to the floor.

"I know how you feel, but everything is going to be just fine as long as we stick together, I promise," said Xavier.

After watching him pout and pack, Xavier agreed to let him at least say his goodbyes to his friends—and then off to Georgia, of all places.

They finally settled down in Augusta and rented a house from an old friend who was sent to Germany for overseas duty.

Xavier got a job, and Czun got settled in their new house. After years of moving from town to town, unpacking was a cinch. Czun unpacked and organized the house, even though he knew they would be moving again in a few months.

One day after work, Xavier called Czun out to the car.

"I know that this move wasn't the easiest thing for you, but I just want to say that you are the best thing that has ever happened to me and I love you. Happy birthday," said Xavier, pulling the tarp off the trailer hooked up to the 4 Runner, revealed a brand-new Honda Shadow.

"Thanks, Dad! How did you know how bad I really wanted a motorcycle?" Czun asked.

"Well, when I was your age, I wanted the same thing, not to mention all the pictures on your walls and the riding lessons you were sneaking from your friends behind my back. I admit you ride well enough to have a bike. You are not allowed to ride late at night, and you are for no reason allowed to have anyone on the back, and no speeding," demanded Xavier

"Can I go for a ride now?" Czun beamed with excitement.

"Practice the riding test in the parking lot and tonight study for the written test. We'll go down to the DMV tomorrow. If you pass, then you can ride as much as you want—as long as you stay out of trouble," warned Xavier.

Later that night, Xavier came into Czun's room and gave him the bad news.

"I know how much you have enjoyed this little vacation, but it's time for you to enroll in school. That gives you the rest of the weekend to enjoy the bike; if you get your permit." Xavier smiled.

Czun smiled back at Xavier. In a way, he was eager to make new friends. Although, sometimes he got kind of nervous. He thought that people would think he looked weird and wouldn't like him. The thought passed through his mind quickly as he prepared for tomorrow's test.

Early Saturday morning Xavier fixed their breakfast, and like clockwork, he smelled the sweet smell of food and wandered into the kitchen.

"Good morning, Czun. Did you sleep well?" asked Xavier.

"No, not really, I tossed and turned all night thinking about my bike. When can we go to the test place?" he asked.

"We can go after breakfast if you like," said Xavier.

"Cool!" smiled Czun.

The two finished breakfast and headed to the DMV. After waiting in line for what seemed to be an eternity, Czun passed both the written and riding test with flying colors.

He looked at Xavier. "Can I go out riding for a little while before we go home?"

"Sure, kid, but I want you home before dark," Xavier replied.

Czun hopped on the bike and rode down the street. It was the end of summer and the hot sun, and the cool breeze made today a good day for riding. He looked up ahead and saw a straight-away with not a car in sight, so he revved up the throttle and zoomed down the road. The adrenaline rushed through his veins like a wild river. He felt the power of the bike flow through him. He snapped back to his senses and slowed down at the end of the strip. He calmed down and look back at the road. He felt a cool draft all over his body. He felt an odd chill. Then he noticed that his shirt was stretched out and ripped, and his pants were torn and unsnapped.

"I must have lost control of myself; I can't let that happen again. Dad will be pissed if I don't get home soon," Czun said to himself.

His ride home was both cool and refreshing. He made it into the house without Xavier noticing.

As Czun started to change clothes, Xavier walked into his room looking very upset.

"Where have you been? There has been some kind of mass murder at the school you were about to go to. They say that some of the bodies were ripped apart, totally mutilated. Where did you go today, and why are your clothes torn?" Xavier leered at Czun waiting for a really good explanation.

"I just went riding. I don't know exactly where I was— you think I did that to those people?" he replied. defensively

"Well I want to believe you, but you sneak in the house with torn clothes on. What am I supposed to think? You are the only one I know who could do this type of thing and not leave a witness," Xavier said.

"The truth is I was going a little fast on the bike, and I got excited and started to change, but I calmed down before anyone could see me and I definitely didn't go to any schools. Besides if I killed all those people don't you think I would have blood on my clothes?" replied Czun.

"You're right, I guess; sorry I accused you. I guess that knowing what you're capable of made me assume you were guilty. Take a shower, grab some leftovers, and go to bed— we will talk in the morning." Xavier started dialing numbers on his phone as he walked out of Czun's room.

Czun did as he was told, with a frown on his face. He knew that Xavier believed him, but to accuse him in the first place really hurt.

Sunday rolled around, and Czun spent the day riding around town, trying to find a place to hang out. He found a motorcycle shop and used Xavier's credit to buy a motorcycle jumpsuit. He bought it a few sizes too large just in case he changed again. He then spent the rest of the afternoon trying to find his way home.

It was Monday morning. Czun woke up to a big breakfast.

"Good morning, son. I have good news and bad news; which do you want first?" asked Xavier.

"The bad," he exclaimed sleepily.

"Okay, then the bad news is the school you were supposed to go to is closed due to an ongoing investigation. The good news is you get to attend a different school until the other one reopens," smiled Xavier.

Czun looked over at Xavier. "You have the good news and bad news thing confused, by the way. What time does school start?"

"I have to take care of some business this morning. The directions are on the counter. You have to meet with the principal around eight; that gives you an hour and a half to get dressed and find your way to Brewer High." Xavier pointed at the counter with a mischievous smile.

Czun finished his meal and looked at the directions. Going to a new school wasn't new for him. He had been going from school to school since he left the jungle.

"For some reason, I have a good feeling about this state and this school. I felt a comfort in knowing that we might stay here for a while. It's time to go," he said to himself as he walked out the door, putting on his helmet.

After a few wrong turns here and there, he finally reached the school.

Looking at his watch, he said, "Fifteen minutes, not bad." He walked to the front of the school.

The students were standing around the halls and outside of lockers waiting for the bell to ring. Most of the students who were not absorbed in conversation turned to look at Czun.

He was used to it by now: the stares on his back, the whispers they thought he couldn't hear, breezing around his head. He ignored them and finally found the principal's office. Inside the office, the principal made his introduction speech and welcomed Czun to the school.

Principal Markus was a tall man, balding in the front with long hair in the back. He looked like a hippie still trying to hold on to the old days.

As the morning dragged on, Czun pretended to be on a mighty adventure of finding his classes. The goal was to do so before the bell, so as not to draw any more attention to himself. When all of a sudden wham!

"Hey dumb ass, watch where you're going," a big building of a guy yelled down.

"My bad," Czun replied.

"You're damn right it's your bad. Do you know who I am?" Harlequin asked.

"As far as I can tell, you are a bus parked inside a school, so I'm guessing they call you school bus?" Czun said with a chuckle, making all the students laugh with him.

"You're funny. Let's see you laugh with no teeth," said Harlequin as he swung at Czun.

He stepped out of the way, grabbing his arm and flipping him to the floor.

"I learned that from a karate movie," Czun said with a cocky smirk.

The next thing Czun knew, he was sitting back in the principal's office explaining what was going on.

"There is no one at your home number—do you have another number, where I can call your guardian?" asked Principal Markus.

"That depends—what time is it? If it's around noon he's at a little bar on the corner named O'REILLY'S PUB." said Harlequin, leaning back in the chair, getting comfortable.

From the conversation between the principal and Harlequin, he'd been in the chair many times before.

Czun, on the other hand, felt as though he could use a sedative. Hot flashes and cold sweats consumed his body as the principal asked for the number of his father. Czun gave Xavier's cell phone number, hoping that he wouldn't be able to receive the call. But no luck; the teacher had a couple of words with Xavier and then hung up. The principal looked over at Czun and smiled.

"Good news; your father will be here in a few minutes. It seems he was already on the way because you forgot your license." Principal Markus frowned. "As for you, Mr. Harlequin, since there is no way of contacting your legal guardian again, then we are going to contact your probation officer. It will be recommended that your case be taken to social services. Maybe in a few months, you will prove that you can join your peers without resorting to violence," said Principal Markus with a look of disappointment.

"Back to you, Mr. Czun. You will be suspended for the rest of the day. I hope you start tomorrow off better than you did today, because if I see you in my office again, I will not be as lenient." With that, Mr. Markus opened the door and directed the two boys to the hallway.

16

A few minutes seemed like days as Czun waited for Xavier. Finally, Xavier walked into the office. He glared at Czun as if he were a serial killer and then turned his attention to Principal Markus.

"Is everyone all right?" Xavier inquired

"That's an odd question, seeing that the other boy is almost twice your son's size, but yes, both boys are fine. As a matter of fact, I witnessed most of the confrontation. I must say, your son is pretty brave for standing up to such a big guy," Markus replied

"You should be teaching that it takes more courage to walk away from a fight rather than patting them on the back for starting one!" Xavier replied with anger in his voice. "Get your stuff, and let's go!"

Czun grabbed his books and headed outside.

Xavier pointed at the trailer hitched to the back. "Put your bike back here; you are forbidden to ride until further notice. I will take you to school from now on," Xavier said.

"I don't think so; I would rather walk than to have you holding my hand back and forth to school like I was some kind of baby!" Czun shouted rebelliously.

There was silence all the way home; neither of them would put aside his pride to work things out. Pride had always been a barrier between them, and it might continue to be for some time to come. Usually one of them broke down, and they became the best of friends and even a family again; but for now, they were locked in their own world of egotism.

Dinner time rolled around, and Czun skipped out on the meal to stay in his room and sulk for a while longer. Xavier went to his room and looked in on his son as he usually did before he went to bed.

"Good night, son," Xavier said as he passed by.

"Yeah." Czun exclaimed in a short and abrupt tone.

He listened to Xavier's heart begin to slow and heard him start to snore.

Sitting up in bed, Czun pondered about sneaking out.

First, he walked to the kitchen, figuring if he got caught, he would say he was fixing a late snack because he missed dinner. Having a second listen, he heard Xavier sound asleep.

Czun whispered to himself, "I am as free as a bird." As he stepped out the door, he kicked off his shoes and shirt. The warm breeze and the dark midnight sky reminded him of a home so far back in his memory it seemed like a dream. He began to change into his true form, but only partly. He shifted just enough not to reveal his true self to the nosy neighbors. He began to run, faster and faster; his muscles started to grow and strengthen. He grimaced with joy at the feeling of the ground pounding under his feet and the wind in his face. He took a small leap, landing gently on the roof of a house and then pouncing into a tree and scaling it with ease, higher and higher. He did a somersault and flipped from tree to tree, going deeper into the small wooded area between the housing complexes.

He reached the end of the woods and dropped to the ground. He squatted on the ground, breathing deeply to slow down his adrenaline-pumping heart.

F lashing lights appeared around a house in the distance. When the police come on over the intercom, machine guns blared, and two cops fell to the ground covered in blood. The other officers scurried like roaches in a lighted room.

"Wow, there are cop cars everywhere," Czun whispered to himself.

The number of people in the house was unknown, but the fire-power in there was definitely more significant than the police.

Czun decided to step into action, covering himself from head to toe with fur and unleashing his fangs and claws.

With a howl in the night sky, he ran and flipped from the roof of the police car to the roof of the house, punching through the roof quicker than the police spotlight could get a fix on him.

Inside the attic, he heard at least six people reloading their weapons. He scratched a hole through the ceiling to see what he was up against.

It was dark in the room they were held up in, but Czun could see perfectly. He looked around and noticed another six in the kitchen. He heard one man in the bedroom giving orders to the small army.

He looked down again, and there was a man with a big gun. It seemed like he was loading little missiles into it.

"The time is now or never!" he said to himself as he burst through the ceiling. He growled and snapped at the guy with the missile. He knocked him out with one punch. Then he pounced on another guy. Guns started to fire.

"Wow," he said to himself. He could see the bullets as they came out of the gun, but there were too many of them to dodge. "Why aren't I dead? The bullets are sticking to my fur," he murmured to himself, looking down.

He ran through the men as if they were nothing. A couple of them ran out with their hand up choosing to face the cops than Czun. The other men, freaked out by his appearance, began to shoot wildly and hit each other with stray bullets. The leader proving that he was a coward, tried to hide when he heard the screams of his men. Czun found him and dragged him from under the bed. He picked him up and slammed him to the wall. His heart was beating one hundred miles an hour as he stared at Czun's sharp teeth. Czun raised his claw and punched the wall, missing his head by inches. The man fainted, and Czun tossed him out the door in front of the police.

Czun rammed through the wall on the side of the building. He continued into the thick foliage and bushes, as the cops took cover; disoriented from the exploding wall.

Czun ran into the woods and climbed from tree to tree until he was sure that no one was following him. He then phased off the fur and walked home with a sense of pride from helping out the police.

19

But that was short lived as he reached the porch and noticed Xavier waiting for him outside.

"No matter what I say, you just won't listen, will you? Years ago, you promised me that you would do what I asked. You went back on your word, and tonight you completely crossed the line," yelled Xavier.

"You crossed the line—you put me in a cage when I was just a kid and you have been trying to keep me locked up since then, you treat me like—like—" Czun fumbled for the right words.

"I treat you like what? I have never done anything that would hurt you, and the only reason you are refrained from doing things is that you lack the responsibility to handle yourself in a civilized manner when a tough situation comes along!" Xavier stated.

"Actually, I handled the situation very civilized today; I was provoked. I tried to make light of the situation, and it didn't work. You know, it's not easy being the new kid on the block, especially when you look like me. But you never asked these things; you go straight to the accusations. And for the record, I am not human. I am not part of your society. If I wanted to hurt that boy, I could have killed him, and no one there could have stopped me!" Czun growled these words, then stormed to his room, not noticing that his fangs and claws were starting to show.

Xavier, shaken by the transformation, gave Czun a few minutes to calm down and then walked in after him.

"You know what I hate most about when we argue? It's when you are right, and I have to be man enough to admit it. Maybe I do jump the gun a little. It's just that I see you in a different light—not because you are different, but because your actions remind me of someone who made some bad choices in life. Choices that he will pay for, for the rest of his life. As a matter of fact, the only good thing the guy ever did was adopt you; but that's a story for another day," confessed Xavier. "Listen, son, you did break the rules, and you will be punished for that." Xavier looked sad and disappointed.

"Yeah, I know." He sighed.

"Well, here is the deal; you are grounded for two weeks, one week for the school incident and one week for disappearing tonight, and you are not allowed to ride your motorcycle for one week."

"That sounds fair," he exclaimed.

"Well, I'm glad you approve," Xavier replied sarcastically. "Now go to bed; you have a long walk in the morning unless you want that ride to school."

"I guess I can take that ride if you promise not to hold my hand or give me a goodbye kiss when I get out the car," he said sarcastically.

Xavier turned out the light on his way out and headed back to bed.

Morning came almost too quickly. Xavier gave Czun a wake-up call half an hour earlier than usual.

"Czun, wake up—I have to go into the office early this morning, it seems there was a problem with a business deal last night; they need me in first thing. I hope you don't mind," Xavier yelled down the hall.

"You could let me sleep in—or better yet, you could let me drive my bike," Czun said in a sleepy moan.

Xavier shook his head, ignoring the comment.

Czun washed up and got dressed, then sat at the table for breakfast.

"You know, Dad, you always talk about making good business deals and bad business deals, but you never talk about what it is you actually do," Czun stated.

"Well, I do a lot of different things at the office. From accounting to large claims and business mergers," Xavier said nervously, placing a plate of food in front of him. "Hurry up and eat; we have ten minutes until time to go, and I can't be late."

Czun scarfed his food down, still wandering what Xavier did for a living. He blew it off and took another good look at his hair before walking out the door.

"I don't plan to be late picking you up, but if I do run behind, don't leave and don't get in any trouble," Xavier stated, giving him a small but stern stare while driving.

"I think you worry too much; I'll be fine," he replied.

They pulled up in front of the school, and Czun looked over at Xavier. The look in his eye showed he was plotting something.

"Please don't embarrass me," he begged as he got out of the truck.

Xavier smiled. "Would I do something like that?"

Waiting for him to take a few steps away from the truck, he then honked. "Honey, do you have enough lunch money?" Xavier yelled out.

Czun's head dropped down with embarrassment as he turned, smiled, and whispered out to him, "I owe you one." Then he walked to the back of the school.

The back of the school was close to Czun's homeroom; it was also where the in-crowd and the jocks hung out. It was funny how it was like that in every school he had ever been in.

"Dude, what's up?" a nasally-voiced young Hispanic-looking guy called out as he approached Czun. "My name is Luis. I saw you yesterday in the hall. Man, that was cool; that guy was like the school bully, and he had you pegged as a punk as soon as you got off your bike. Where is your bike? You are supposed to park around here in the back. Teachers park in front; freshmen aren't allowed to drive to school. Sophomores park on the west and juniors and seniors park on the east and around the back. By the way, what the hell are you?"

"What do you mean, what am I?" Czun tensed, feeling that maybe his secret was finally let out of the bag.

"I mean what are you—a freshman, sophomore, junior, or senior?" Luis asked.

"I was a junior, but since I changed schools, I was put back a semester, so I guess I am a sophomore and a half I'm in Mrs. Mathews's homeroom with sophomores," Czun replied thinking to himself, *This guy sure talks a lot.* He looked Hispanic, but he didn't have an accent. He reminded Czun of one of those guys who tried too hard to make friends, and it turned out to work in reverse.

"I'm a sophomore too; we might have some of the same classes. What are your courses?" Luis rambled on.

"Well here are the courses I'm supposed to be taking, but I am going to switch this agriculture thing for home economics."

"Home ec? why would you trade off a semester of easy A's in the great outdoors to be cooped up inside baking cookies with a bunch of fat snobbish girls?" asked Luis, looking almost disgusted with Czun.

"Well, think of it this way—how can a new guy get to meet girls and get to make a lot of female friends, and also be known as Mr. Sensitive and caring with practically no effort?"

"I never thought of it that way. I think I'll try to get home ec too. What period are you taking it?"

"I'm going to try to take it fifth period. That way I can eat snacks. It's a long time between lunch periods and getting home, you know," Czun said, rubbing his belly. "Now it's time for my favorite part of the morning," Czun told Luis.

Luis, having lived here all his life, made jokes as he pointed out the snobs and the nerds of the school. It was funny how he never mentioned what category he fell into, although it was easy to tell by the way he dressed and talked. Czun listened and made no comment; who was he to judge people on their appearance?

Luis then began to point out the girls who had boyfriends or girlfriends at the end of summer. The school grounds soon got crowded as the buses unload the kids like cattle.

"What time do they start letting us in to get to class?" Czun asked his new sidekick, Luis.

Just then, the bell rang.

"Seven-thirty on the dot; you can set an alarm to it. As a matter of fact, you should if you don't want to be late for your classes; two tardy sheets and you get an hour of detention," Luis warned.

Hundreds of kids pour into the school to find their lockers, their classes, and most of all, their friends. This made it harder for Czun to find his way around, but he eventually got to his classes. Listening as he walked down the halls, a lot of the kids and teachers were talking about his dramatic first day at school. The students were standoffish, not sure if he was a troublemaker. The teachers were sure he was a troublemaker. Either way, everyone kept their distance.

Lunch rolled around, and Czun sat alone in a small table in a corner.

"Dude, what's up?" Luis said popping up from behind. "Man, everyone is talking about you! Girls are pointing you out; even the teachers are mentioning you in their classes. It's like you are some kind of celebrity. What do you have for fourth period?"

"I have English. The teacher is—Mrs. Hatney," he said, fumbling through his back pocket to look at his schedule

"Me too, that means we have fourth and fifth period together." Luis beamed.

"What do you mean, fourth and fifth together?"

"Well, what you said about home ec made sense, so I decided to follow your advice. I also want to watch you in action, just to see if you are as smooth as you say."

Luis and Czun scarfed down their meals and headed outside for fresh air. The sky was overcast, so they weren't pressured to find a shady spot. They worked their way toward the door of the school closest to their lockers. Czun leaned against the wall trying to look cool, dreading the fact that the bell would ring at any minute.

A couple of girls walked up to Luis. "Hi, Luis. You going out for track this year?" Carla asked, staring down Czun like he was fresh meat.

"Yeah, I talked to the coach before lunch, and he said try-outs start next month," Luis answered, only to be ignored.

"So, who's your friend?" Angelica asked, no longer able to sit through the small talk.

"Oh, he's nobody," he said, nodding his head at Czun, knowing that the two girls knew who he was, but still letting them play their game.

"What, he can't speak for himself?" Carla replied, looking at Luis as if he were beneath her.

"Hello, my name is Czun. Don't mind my friend Luis; I told him how beautiful you two were as you were walking by and how shy I am around ladies. He was just looking out for me," Czun replied with a slight smile.

"You're afraid to talk to us?" Carla asked.

"No, not afraid. I'm not afraid of anything, I said I was shy—sometimes, anyway. If I were afraid, I would have left before I saw your chocolate-brown eyes," Czun continued, smiling a little more. He knew that even his corniest lines would work on these two.

The bell rang, signaling the end of lunch

"Well, ladies, it was nice meeting you, but I have to find my way to Mrs. Hatney's English class, and since I don't know my way around, it's going to take me a while to find it." He waited for a response.

"Oh, well—we are walking that way," said Carla.

"We can walk you to class," Angelica said, cutting Carla short.

"That would be great, but I don't want you to be late for your classes because of me. Besides, this will give me a chance to do a little guy talk with Luis and find out a little about you guys." Czun waved, turned, and walked to class.

Luis smiled; he was happy to be included in the conversation with the new coolest guy in school.

Eventually, the classes came to an end, and school was over. Czun met up with Luis in the front of the school.

"What's up? You want a ride home? My father will be here in a few minutes," Czun offered.

"Sure. I hate riding with all those rowdy freshmen."

"Where do you live?"

"I live on the other side of Tobacco Road, near the old public pool." Luis pointed as if it were across the street.

"Even better. That's on our way; we live off Tobacco Road on the right side of Windsor Spring Road."

Time passed, and the two boys were still waiting on Xavier to drive up.

"Hey man, If I'm not home before my mom to have the house clean, I'm gonna be in deep crap," Luis said, looking a little nervous and anxious.

"I'm really sorry, dude; my dad is hardly ever late. Let's go find a phone and call him. There is a Circle K up the road, and if he passes by, we can flag him down," Czun said, trying to put his worried friend's mind at ease.

Halfway to the store, Xavier drove up.

"Hi, Dad. This is Luis; he's in my class. Can we give him a ride?" Czun asked with a sweet and innocent look on his face.

"No! Let him walk!" Xavier bellowed rudely and abruptly, then smiled. "Zikes!" he said with a smile. "Sure, he can have a ride. Where do you live?" Xavier laughed.

"Thank you, sir." Luis sighed with relief.

After they dropped off Luis, Xavier let Czun have it. "You know before you offer anyone a ride you should first clear it with their parents, so it doesn't look like I kidnapped someone's child."

"Is there something bothering you, Dad? You seem a little upset. If I knew that there would be a problem with giving my friend a ride, I never would have offered," he apologized.

"No, that's not it; there was a problem at one of the factories last night. There was a break-in, and a lot of the merchandise got stolen and destroyed. We can't get any support from the insurance because a lot of the paperwork was destroyed in the theft."

"That's terrible. Did the cops catch the thief?"

"No, the police don't have a clue who broke in. They think it was an inside job."

"By the way, the word is psych, not zikes, but it was a really cool attempt." Czun smirked.

At the house, Czun got started on his homework as Xavier prepared for dinner.

"Czun, I have to go to the office for a few hours tonight, so don't wait up for me. Oh, and you can ride your bike to school tomorrow, but remember, no one is allowed on the back of that thing. Are we clear on that?" Xavier spoke in a firm voice.

"Cool, thanks, Dad; you picked up major cool points tonight."

After dinner, Xavier headed off to work, and Czun felt like stretching out his paws.

He put on a pair of his baggiest pants and a loose t-shirt and headed for the woods.

"Think I want to work on my speed and backflips tonight," he said to himself.

After about an hour of handstands, he took a break and listened to the cool wind blow. In the distance, he heard sirens.

"Cool, some action," he mumbled aloud as he ran to the action.

Two miles up the road, Czun spotted the police cars doing another drug bust, but this time the drug dealers were in a huge factory.

Czun saw an open window about thirty feet up; he ran and jumped for it. Grabbing the windowsill, he tucked and curled inside in virtual silence. He looked down into the factory and spotted a familiar face.

"Hello, Harlequin. Well, it's time to take out the garbage," Czun whispered to himself, tying his now shoulder-length hair tightly to the back.

There were at least seven heavily armed men. All prepared to attack when the police rushed. The gunfight began. The entire place was mass chaos; the police and drug dealers ran for cover to dodge each other's bullets. Suddenly, Czun heard a distinct voice—it was Xavier, caught in the crossfire.

He leaped down almost on top of Xavier, throwing him over his shoulder, and retreated to a corner of the factory away from the commotion.

"What are you doing here? You were supposed to be at the office?" he asked, morphing his face to look more human, and showing his confusion.

"Well, there is something that I have to tell you that you aren't going to like. You see, in order for us to live in peace without having to run to a different state from the—let's call them the mob—I had to do a few jobs and repay my debt. Last night would have been my last night doing this, but the place was raided and demolished by the time I got there," explained Xavier

"Hey, what the hell? Harlequin said watching a man and a monster talking in the corner. "You double-crossing asshole—die, bitch!"

Harlequin shot; bullets streamed everywhere. Czun grabbed Xavier and ran for safety. Finally making it to the outside, Czun felt something wet running down his fur. It was Xavier. He'd been hit, and he was dying.

"Czun, listen to me; all I ever wanted to do was make things easy for us. I wanted to make a good life for myself at first. Then you came along, and all I wanted to do was make things good for you. That's what a good father would do for his son."

"Don't talk, Dad. If I can concentrate hard enough, I can make it to the hospital quickly," Czun whispered.

"No, Czun; it's too late. Besides, they will be waiting for us there and at home. I have a safety deposit box with both our names on it. Inside is two thousand dollars, and power of attorney to other bank accounts—thirty in all, under different names. Each should have at least one hundred thousand in them. Take the truck and—"

Then there was silence. Xavier's expression was blank as he stared at Czun; his soul was gone.

"Father, Father! No—no!" Czun yelled with rage. His t-shirt ripped, his jeans split apart as he walked back into the factory. The police were pinned back, waiting for the SWAT team. The beast didn't notice them, but he did see Harlequin and charged at him. The other gang members tried to hold the beast back, but to no avail. The bullets barely penetrated his thick fur and tough skin. The beast lashed and tore the men apart. It was a massacre. All that crossed his path were killed; some died slower than others.

The police found Xavier's body later that night.

Czun calmed down and sat in an alley with blood drenched on what was left of his clothes. He started to dig bullets from under his skin. Wedged in like splinters, they didn't hurt, but they were annoying.

The sky was cloudy, and there was no light in the alley; the stench of death started to tickle his nose. His attention was drawn to the other end of the alley where he saw a figure lurking in the shadows.

"Who's there?"

"The last person you will ever see, you blood-sucking dog," said the voice as it came charging at Czun.

Czun tightens his hair back in preparation for the attack. The shadowed attacker moved quickly, and Czun was almost cut by one of the long knives the attacker was wielding.

"You must have been dead for a while to dodge that. No matter; you are still going down. You will never kill again after tonight."

"How did you know about tonight? Who are you?" Czun asked, blocking and countering the attacker's every move.

"To you I am death; the rest shouldn't matter!"

Czun was really getting pissed at this guy's Batman vigilante mumbo-jumbo and decided to put the attacker down. He morphed out just

ROB BATTLE

enough to get the upper hand and disarm the attacker. Czun grabbed him by the throat and slammed him to the wall.

"I'll ask you again, who are you?" Czun growled

"You aren't a ghoul; what the hell are you?"

"I ask the questions, you answer them. That's if you want to continue breathing," he said, squeezing the attacker's throat tighter.

"Have it your way!" the attacker said, placing his hand on Czun's shoulder.

Czun felt a weakness come over him. He dropped to one knee, still holding on to the throat of the attacker.

"My name is Gerald," he said, pulling Czun's hand from his neck. "I smell death on you, and I thought you were a ghoul. I have to destroy them before they band together and go on a killing spree like they did in my school."

"You are the one behind that massacre?"

"No, I stopped the massacre before it got worse. Now I gotta find the others. Why're you covered in blood?" he asked.

"I was stopping a drug deal," Czun said with a tone of remorse.

"Well, it seems we are on the same team. Here, take my jacket," Gerald offered.

"Thanks. Where are you heading?" Czun asked.

"Back to my hotel. I have a police scanner I use to get me my leads; that's how I found you."

"Well, you are welcome to come to my place, after I get rid of the thugs who are waiting for me," Czun smirked.

"Sounds like fun," Gerald replied, thinking, *I know what he is going through. He shouldn't be alone at a time like this, regardless of how he may seem on the outside.*

28

Gerald and Czun walked the shadows all the way home trying not to be noticed. They told each other of the events that led to their chance meeting. After some thought, Czun decided to help Gerald on his quest.

They reached the house just before dawn and spotted a car casing the house.

"That must be the drug dealers. Wait here, and I'll take care of them. Wait here!" Czun directed Gerald as if he were a child.

"No, I have a better idea, because if you go over there you'll have to kill them and more will return. Let me try something," Gerald requested.

"Go ahead, but I will be close just in case." Czun put his trust in this total stranger and had no reason why.

Gerald walked up to the car and poked his head inside.

"Hi. If you are looking for Czun, he's dead. You can go on in peace now." Gerald put his hand on the driver's shoulder and drained just enough essence to put him to sleep. In the morning, the car was gone.

Months passed; Czun and Gerald built a bond of kinship. Czun helped Gerald hunt for ghouls.

Occasionally, Gerald needed to feed on the essence of the living to survive. He chose to go out alone for this. Regardless of how much good Gerald did, this seemed like an evil deed. That was why he fed only on criminals—or rather, people who were committing crimes.

After a couple of months, Czun decided to go back to school. With the prior training from Xavier; Czun doctored up more transfer papers and use them as a cover to return to high school as his friend Luis.

Gerald studied some college courses at home once in a while. He did not ever, ever want to step back into another school if he could help it.

PART 5
Grey: The Bridge between The Dark and The Light

1

"Gerald, you have been talking for a while now. If you don't mind, I would like to tell my own story. Sitting here listening to you ramble on is getting quite boring." A voice chimed into Gerald, Lilly, and Zarian's link.

"Maybe we should ask them, Grey," Gerald said cautiously. "Why don't you link through me to them. So, if something goes wrong, no one gets hurt—except me."

Lilly got up and refilled her cup of coffee. She looked at the clock on her desk. Only twenty minutes had passed. How was that possible? She just relived the stories of two lifetimes.

Noticing her confusion, Zarian spoke. "My friend, are you okay?"

"Uh, I don't know. It feels like more time has gone by, but it hasn't. It felt like I was living each day with G- and Czun, but it has only been twenty minutes." Her face showed all the confusion she felt.

"Well, my friend, your mind is faster than your actions. Kind of like fast forward on your VHS," Zarian explained.

Lilly smiled then sat back down. "Okay, let's do this."

"My brother Grey is new at the telepathy thing. We are working on it, but sometimes he pushes his way in and it causes headaches. That is why I will be a buffer, but he will be the one to tell his tale." Gerald put out a caution. "Oh, and don't call me G, Ger, Gerry, or any other nickname. Gerald is a good name, thank you. Grey, you're up," he continued, not giving anyone a chance for rebuttal.

"Thank you, big brother."

Grey began his tale.

2

"**D**eath caught me by surprise. This was the story of my life. Before I go any further, you should know two things. First, you should know this is a horror story—and second, as you have heard, I am dead."

"So, how does a dead guy tell a story? Well, that is what makes this a horror story." I sat down on the roof of the building Gerald, Lilly, and Zarian were in. I looked over in the distance and barely caught a glimpse of Czun weaving through shadows. He was keeping a vigilant watch over the area. What a good watchdog.

I felt Lilly laugh.

"Grey, concentrate," Gerald reprimanded.

I got comfortable and continued. My brothers were calling out to me. I felt the weight of their voices trying to pull me from the black. For the first time, I felt the true power of the black. I knew there was something beyond it, as if the black were only a curtain. There was something there—energy—it pulled me, forcing me to it, like a moth to a flame.

Something instinctual, something primitive and powerful ordered me to come, and I must obey.

So how did I die? I knew that you wouldn't ask such a heartless question, but I will get to that. So, I will tell you how I lived. I will tell you about my brothers from different mothers, different fathers—but still, we are Sons of Darkness.

I felt my brothers fighting for their lives, and they were losing. I could tell they wanted to mourn me, but there was no time. I was there with them, but far away. It felt like I was in a dark phone booth floating in space. I heard everything that was happening. I saw it in the back of my mind as if it were a video, but I wasn't there.

Someone screamed? I felt the bloody gash on Gerald's back throbbing with pain. It was a numbing feeling. Like people who had lost limbs describe their missing part.

He was crawling on the ground toward Czun. Czun was in full battle mode. We all knew that when Czun was like that it was fight or flight; so best to stay out of his way. For Gerald to get so near to him now meant that he would rather risk friendly fire than the alternative. God help them.

"Aaaaahhhhhh, somebody help them!" My screams were unheard.

A figure in a dark cloak grabbed Gerald by the foot as he tried to crawl closer to Czun. He picked Gerald up like a rag doll and slammed him to the floor.

Gerald let out a gasp and tried to roll away. He stuck his arm out to soften the blow. It was a costly sacrifice to stick his arm out like that. The bone sticking out made his arm crease in a way it was not meant to.

Blood loss would be a bad thing for a vampire, but Gerald was different. Yeah, he had fangs and claws, but he didn't drink blood. He consumed energy or essence—not sure which. I am not even sure how he did it. You wouldn't ask an addict how he did the drug; besides, his pride didn't allow him to explain.

This was how I knew he was in serious trouble. His pride wouldn't allow him to ask for the help from his little brother. Although right now his baby brother was about three times his size. That was him there covered in fur—um, with the tail.

My youngest brother is Czun, pronounced Jun. I know it was a weird name; he claimed it was an ancient name of royalty and power. I thought he was full of czit, but since he was the only one we knew of that spoke his native language, we never called him on it.

Czun had been in his primal wolf form (that's what he calls it) only twice that I can recall. He almost killed Gerald and me, and it was easy for him. When he was like that, he wasn't a man at all. He was wounded, a caged animal, and it was fight or flight. Gerald and I made the mistake of blocking his flight, and he made it a short fight.

All that power in a fifteen-year-old boy. No wonder he looked at us humans like we were either food or pets. It was cool that he never treated us like that, though. I guess he treated people like he wanted to be treated.

He was covered in blood, fighting for survival. He was overpowered by my father's army of the unclean, unholy filth. He was surrounded by Helen's clan of the undead. My once proud brother who lived for a good fight would soon be beside me in death.

How did we get here? I could say it was our fate. How will it end? That was our destiny.

I think I need to go back a little and tell you about who I am.

Theoretically speaking, if life is represented as white and death is represented by black, then it would only be fitting that my name be Grey.

Another school day had ended, and as I biked home, I felt sad. The kids at school always teased me and called me names. The worst was burnt charcoal, I didn't even know what that meant. What was burnt charcoal? They called me a punk because I was so tall for my age, but I didn't play sports. The coach wanted me to play football because I was powerful for my age.

"Holy crap, I am sixteen today! Happy birthday to me," I sang to myself.

It was the only happy birthday I would hear. We didn't celebrate my birthday. My father didn't even acknowledge I had a birthday. Since I had no other family or real friends, today was just another day, yet somehow sadder.

Father had already gone to work when I got home. He left a nice chore list for me, and it all had to be done today. As night fell, I looked up at the moon. It was so round and bright that you could see the craters in it. I felt the cool November breeze creep through my jacket, and I knew that it was going to be a cold night. I was in a hurry, because I wanted to be done before dark, but apparently, it didn't happen.

It was Thursday, and I always tended Mother's grave on Thursdays, rain or shine. She died giving birth to me on a Thursday. Although I never got to know her, Thursdays seemed to be our day.

While I pulled weeds and scrubbed her headstone, I felt a numbing pain shoot through my chest and out of my hands. Trying to catch my breath, I stood up.

I heard a woman's voice. "Grey, you are in danger. I have escaped from your father's grasp." Her voice was whispered and panicked.

"You are in danger physically and spiritually. I was enslaved by your father for a long time."

"Who are you? What kind of sick joke are you playing in a cemetery?" I yelled.

"Your father knew that I would never love an evil man like him. He killed me and brought me back as a zombie. My free will and emotion are buried in an abyss of darkness." The very emotional voice continued. "Unmarried but living as his wife, night after night he took my soulless body and did his will. After many months I became pregnant, hich I found out was his plan all along," she said as her voice grew faint.

"**Y**ou're lying!" I yelled out, looking around, trying to find where the voice was coming from. I felt something deep inside of me, and I knew she was telling the truth.

Then other spirits came about—spirits that claimed that my father had killed them and taken the spirits of their loved ones to attain more power.

"A child born from the undead would have the power of darkness in the world of the night and would be able to bring forth the city of the damned, the sacred Necropolis," Mother said, weeping hauntedly.

As Mother wept, I felt a cold chill sweep through the center of my chest. "You must never use your powers; it would give power to Saban, the darkness that dwells in the Necropolis."

"You are wrong, I don't have powers," I muttered, trying to keep my jaw from shaking. "If I did, I would bring you back to life," I said with a lump in my throat, trying to hold down my tears.

Then another spirit replied, "If you have no power then how are we talking to you?" She had a good point, I thought.

"As you grow, so do your powers. You must suppress them, for the more you use your power, the stronger you make Saban. When Saban gets enough power channeled from earth, then he will bring forth revelation through the coming of the Necropolis." Mother spoke, but her voice faded in and out as if it was bad reception on a radio.

Then she was gone. I screamed and yelled, trying to get her to tell me what to do, but she was gone.

Mother told me that if I reached into the darkness of my soul, my father would kill me and rule the world with the essence of my soul. It was all so weird, so spooky.

"How am I supposed to believe this is happening? It's like I'm in the Twilight Zone or something." Even though I spoke low and to myself, my voice trembled.

Hours later, I returned home and questioned my father about how Mother died. He saw right through me and knew that my powers had started to surface.

"It's about time you make yourself useful. After all this time, my plan is finally coming to light," Father said with an evil sneer on his face.

The silhouette of his tall, slender frame seemed to stretch to the ceiling. His dark complexion appeared to engulf the poorly lit living room. Without warning, he grabbed me by the arm. I fought to get free of his grip, but he was too strong, too powerful. He threw me to the floor and beat me as if I were a stranger breaking into his home. At that moment, I realized I was no longer his son, but an obstacle he had to destroy for his ruthless plan to be successful. It was then I knew the only family I had in this world changed from being Father to Nyhte.

"We can do this two ways," Nyhte said. "You can give in or be taken. I don't need you alive, now that your abilities have surfaced. All I had to do is possess your soul."

Suddenly my mother's spirit intervened. With a burst of blinding light, Nyhte was hurled down the hall. "Run, my son, run!" she yelled.

I pulled myself from the floor and took off. My vision was blurred from the swelling on my head and the tears in my eyes. Out the door and down the road I ran. Tired and hungry, I ran through the marsh and swamp until I reached the main road. I didn't know the name of the main streets because Nyhte felt I didn't need to. I followed the road from the edge of the woods, ducking behind trees every time headlights appeared in the distance. As dawn approached, I was so exhausted that even my shoelaces felt heavy. I walked a few feet deeper in the woods and sat for a while, trying to get my thoughts together. The morning dew mixed with the cold made my lungs burn, and my throat fell scratchy. In the distance, the fog started to roll in as if it was poured from a pitcher.

I woke up. I remember my eyes got heavy, but I couldn't remember how I got on the ground. I felt well rested, and my chest and throat felt better.

"I must be getting used to the cold or in shock," I said to myself, because it dawned on me that I didn't feel anything.

"I must be dead," I muttered.

"Not exactly," a voice responded.

"Who's there? Mother, is that you?" I said, half-dazed, as I looked around.

"I know I'm dead, but do I really sound like a woman?" the voice answered with a thick, playful Louisiana accent.

"No, I guess not," I sighed

"Name's Ty; guess I'm yo guardian spirit, at least fo right now."

"What—where are you?" I asked as I tried to mask the fear in my voice.

"That's hard to answer; I'm all around you and inside, too. Usually, spirits that ain't crossed over can't even be seen or heard of. But round you, our energy becomes more concentrated. You're a necromancer; you can call up the spirits of lost soul if'n ya want to."

"No, I can't! Even if I knew how, Mother said it would be bad," I warned Ty.

"Really? Well, explain why I'm here. The world looks the same. Anyway, your powers are as much a part of you as the hair on your head. Whether you hide it or style it, that's up to you, but it's still gonna to be there. The more you take care of it, the more manageable it'll be. You're the only one who can decide dat." Ty giggled a little.

"Okay then, I want my mother back!" I demanded.

"It's ain't that simple young'un. Let's just say you ain't got enough hair for that style yet."

"Then I want to see you!" I demanded, again.

At that request, I felt numbness in my chest. I looked at my hands as they began to tingle. I looked back up and saw a faint image of a short, middle-aged, Asian man.

"I pictured you taller," I said jokingly.

7

Months went by, and I found myself walking down a long, dark road. It was June, and the humidity was just at the point of being bearable. I was learning self-defense moves from Ty. He swore he was supposed to have been the next Bruce Lee but died in a car accident. He was a pretty good guy, but his little analogies got kind of old. He wasn't a good actor at all. He always misquoted lines from movies, but at least I wasn't entirely alone.

We were on our way to a homeless shelter to get a meal and a safe place to sleep when I felt the presence of a lost spirit. It was very faint, almost as if it were still alive. I began to walk in its direction, all the while being warned by Ty that this was dangerous and could be a trap from my father. *Maybe it was, or maybe my mother found her way back to me*, I thought. As I drew closer to the house, I was overcome by a strong sense of belonging. I felt that I would be at peace with whomever or whatever dwelt in the house. So, I rang the doorbell, and there stood a strange guy with very sad eyes.

"Can I help you?" the guy asked.

"Hi, my name is Grey. I was passing by, and I was—"

"Look, you have come at a bad time!" the guy said and began to close the door

"No, wait, please—just give me a minute," Grey pleaded.

"Back off," the guy said, now shoving the door.

"I said wait!" I demanded, and the door froze in place without me placing a hand on it.

Then another guy came up from behind me and placed his hand on my shoulder. "Relax, dude," he said calmly.

But I did not listen. Now, very frustrated about not being heard, I grabbed the hand on my shoulder and flipped him to the ground.

In a flash, I was off balance; there was a blur of fur. Then I was lying on my back, getting ready to be clawed by a ferocious animal. The second guy yelled out, "Stop! There is something about him. It's like I know him, but we have never met."

"Well, he has a bad way of trying to get acquainted, almost deadly," said the beast.

"Let him speak," requested the guy. "Please get up. Excuse my friend; he is very protective of his territory. My name is Gerald, and he is Czun. Who are you, and what do you want?" Gerald asked in a soft, calm tone.

"My name is Grey, and yours is the spirit I felt. But you are still alive, but your spirit is so faint, as if you are dying, or you are dead but still alive."

"How did you know that?" asked Gerald.

"Well, it's my curse; I am a necromancer," I told them.

Gerald invited me in, but Czun was a little leery about my company. We stayed up all night talking. I told them my whole life story, as if they were shrinks, and they gave me something I never had: friendship.

I decided to live with them. Maybe with these guys around, my father would let me live in peace.

8

It had been two months since we joined together. Czun was in high school; he thought it was a blast to hang out with humans his age, so I joined him. I thought it might be better if I use Czun's last name to keep my father off my trail.

At only sixteen years old, I thought I was the most mature of the group, probably because I never got the chance to play or act my age growing up. I always worked or slept all my life. My father was training me in the culture and arts of Saban. Saban was supposed to be the country where my father was from, although no one had ever heard of it.

I had developed strange new powers, along with the ability to talk with the spirits of the dead. My spiritual guide Ty has moved on. I found that most souls who came around only stayed for a few days, although Ty for some reason remained for a few months. I had discovered that I was telepathic and could place subliminal messages in the minds of others.

Gerald had telepathic abilities also, but his were far more developed than mine. For reasons unknown, Gerald's ability to drain my essence didn't work. That was what he was trying to do the day we met, when he touched my shoulders.

With his beastly strength, supernatural speed, and agility, Czun was a great asset to the team. As Gerald continued to exist and to feed, his powers grew and morphed. He recently learned that he could teleport short distances. He explained it as seeing where you want to be in your mind, and then just being there. He was limited to as far as he could see. Put together with his martial arts skill, Gerald's attack was super deadly, especially for ghouls.

I watched my new brothers and the way they practiced day after day, developing their skills. I felt like I was outclassed. I wanted to learn more of my abilities, but if I did, the evil that could be unleashed was too scary to chance. Besides, if I tried, my father would find me or try to hurt my friends to get to me.

Most mornings when Czun and I got up and had breakfast, Gerald would be just getting in. He usually made a joke or two and called us nerds. I could feel Gerald's hidden resentment because Czun and I had the opportunity to finish school. I could tell he would have wanted to go back to school. His need for essence was aggravated more in the daylight, and the risk of being seen as a semi-ghoul was too dangerous. So, like a true child of the night, Gerald slept all day in a room painted black with the windows covered over.

At night he was as wild and mischievous as any teenage boy. Gerald's condition made him feel like one of the ghouls he chased. Many nights he went out alone, sometimes for hours, looking for a criminal to feed on. I think he fed on criminals to make his guilt more bearable.

It was funny how we all seemed to mesh. I mean I had nothing to contribute to the house. I had no money, but they treated me as an equal, maybe because at six feet three inches I towered over them both.

Czun and I made jokes about being the dynamic duo, fighting crime at night and being mild-mannered students by day—well, at least I was mild-mannered. We hid our powers pretty well, but Czun was awesome when it came to knowing when he could and couldn't change. I had seen him morph his entire arm and no one even noticed.

Czun was quite the ladies' man, while I was awkward when it came to girls. Some of the students steered clear of me; they found me a little weird. It's just human nature to fear death, and that's what I represented, in a manner of speaking.

But there was a particular girl in class named Dawn, a Goth chick, sort of an outcast living in her own world. It was weird, but for some odd reason, Dawn and I seemed to click. I could never get up the nerve to ask her out. I was too shy, I guess.

"What's up, pimp daddy?" Czun walked up to me in between class sessions.

"Hey, Czun, what haven't you been up to?"

"Me, I'm making a date for Friday with Angelica. Why don't you bring Dawn along and we can double?"

"No thanks, I have a 'just be friends' policy with women."

10

"What! You are always talking about how exotic and sexy she looks, and now you say you don't date?" Czun paused and looked at me with astonishment. "You're afraid; you don't want to be turned down. For a quiet guy, you sure have a big ego," laughed Czun

"It's not that at all. I think she is very pretty, but if I ask her out, I think it would change things between us, and so, I know she would say—"

"Yes, I would say yes if you asked me out Friday," Dawn blurted out. "I overheard what you said, and you are the sweetest guy I ever met. I gotta hurry to class. Here's my number; call me tonight." Dawn wrote her number on my forearm and darted off.

"You knew she was back there, didn't you?" I asked with a stern look on my face.

"Nice penmanship; you can tell a lot about a woman who writes across your arm. Gotta go, don't want to be late for gym. I need a good workout. See you after school." Czun sped off to class.

The bell rang, and Czun was in the nick of time.

"Cutting it close again, Mr. Elje," remarked Coach Lofty.

"Not really; I had a five-second grace period until the bell stopped," said Czun in a smart-alecky tone.

"You think you're fast, eh? Well, let's see how fast you are. Everyone go change and meet me on the track in five minutes. Mr. Elje, you have five seconds less," Couch said in the same smart-alecky tone as Czun.

All of the students were on the track except Czun, and the coach was pissed. And then Czun showed up on the track.

"You're late!" the coach yelled.

"No, I'm not. You sent us to change at 2:30 and it's 2:34 and 55 seconds. That's five seconds less, just like you said," smirked Czun

"Well, I say you're late, and you're going to do extra laps after we are done," growled Coach.

"No problem, but I think your slow track team needs it more than me," said Czun in a light but disrespectful tone, causing students to take notice and start snickering.

"So, you say my team is slow? Then why don't you show me."

11

"What's the stakes?" asked Czun.

"What do you mean?" asked the coach.

"Well, I don't do anything just for the fun of it. What's the bet?"

"I'll tell you what; if you win you won't go to the principal's office for smarting off, being disrespectful, and being late, and if you lose, you do three laps on top of that."

"Deal. Who do I race?" beckoned Czun.

"Luis—he's my fastest runner. In fact, he just broke our school record," replied the coach.

"Good thing I'm wearing jogging pants, because I'm going to need a little help," Czun said to himself.

"On your marks, get set, go!" The coach yelled and started his stopwatch.

Czun waited, counted to five, and started running just to prove a point. As the boys raced around the track, Czun morphed from the waist down, just a little so that no one noticed it under his jogging pants. Czun picked up speed, but he didn't want to be too obvious, so he slowed down as he ran neck and neck with Luis.

Luis turned up the juice and gave it his all. "This track is mine, homie!"

"Oh, it's like that, eh?" Czun said to himself and pulled away from Luis, counting to five under his breath.

At the finish line, the students were cheering for Czun and the coach was really steaming now.

"Not only did you beat my star runner, but you broke his record by five seconds, ten if you count that five-second head start you gave him. How did you learn to run like that?" asked the coach with resentment in his voice

"I used to run to the beach every day when I lived in Cali," replied Czun

"Good race, homie," Luis said as he hugged Czun to show good sportsmanship. Luis was always good like that.

Meanwhile, I was not having that good of a last period. First, I was late to class. Then some jock behind me started poking fun at me. I was used to the harassment I got from my peers. Sometimes I laughed with them; it kept the pressure down. Usually, the jokes stopped as the class clowns got bored with me, but not John Myles. He always pushed at my buttons, waiting to get a rise out of me.

Czun confronted me about John messing with me, but I just ignored him. Czun had offered to beat him up for me, but I said no thanks. That would make me look even wimpier —if that's possible.

I knew that I could beat him if it ever came down to a fight, but what would it prove? I would rather let John think he was a tough guy; no one was getting hurt by it. In fact, I got a kick out of being nerdy. It made me feel like Clark Kent from the old *Superman* movies.

For some reason, today the jokes were cutting a little closer to the bone than usual, especially since he had cracked a few jokes about my mother.

"Hey John, why don't you back off today?" I requested. A wrong thing to say to a bully. That meant he was close to getting a rise out of the victim; the jokes and harassment got crueler.

John continued to poke at me, and the class started to laugh louder. I turned forward in my desk and tried to ignore him. John reached up forward and grabbed the back of my shirt and pulled back, causing my collar to choke me. I reached back and grab John's wrist and squeezed it.

"Do you really want to go there?" I murmured as I turned around to John, Looking him in the eyes. John tried to pull away, but he was locked in my grip. "Because that road you are on is long and dark and there is nowhere to turn around."

John was speechless; his mouth was wide open, and a look of genuine fear froze to his face.

I let go of his hand as the teacher walked back in the class.

"Punk," John said under his breath to save face in front of his classmates.

I felt a little glad to be left alone in class, but what would John do after class?

After a long lesson on some guy who I couldn't care less about, the bell rang, and I headed to my locker. I glanced behind me and noticed John walking toward me with his homeboys. As they approached, I found myself wishing that this day had never happened.

John slammed my locker closed. "What's up now, punk?"

"Yeah, what's up now, punk?!" a voice from behind me exclaimed.

I recognized that voice; it was Czun coming to my rescue again.

"Yo man, this fight ain't with you," John replied. His eyes showed that he remembered the fight Czun had with Harlequin months ago. Not to mention the fact that Czun always put out the aura that he was a real tough guy.

"Let me get this straight, you and your sissy friends want to pick on my brother, and you want me to stay out of it. Guess again," Czun said, getting up in John's face.

A crowd started to form as people began to notice the tension building.

"Why are you sweating? There are three of you and two of us," Czun pointed out. "Grey, since John wanted you so bad, you take him, and I will take the other two," Czun said as he stared down the two guys beside John.

John just stood there; I could see his brain wondering if Czun was for real or bluffing. His eyes began to show how quick his bravery was leaving; even his friends began to notice.

"Come on, John, let's go—he ain't worth it," one of the guys said, giving John an exit from the situation he put them in.

"I will catch you later. Don't be alone, punk," John said, trying to save face.

"You know what? If I even hear of anyone messing with my brother, I'm coming for you. Even if you had nothing to do with it. Even if you are out of town. I will find you first, then I will find you and you, then I will find the guy who messed with him. Remember that," Czun said.

John cut his eyes at Czun and walked away.

Czun and I got home from school, and I started dinner. I usually cooked and made sure the bills were paid. Czun cooked once in a while, but no one liked his meals; the meat was either rare or like jerky. Gerald had evolved past eating food; now he thrived only from essence. Once in a while, he ate out of habit, but it made him sick sometimes.

At times it was hard keeping up a good front, but we stuck together no matter what. That way no one would know we had no parents or guardians, and we could stay together without hassle.

Night had fallen, and Gerald was awake. "What's up, guys? How was school?" Gerald asked with a yawn and stretch.

"Same old, same old," I replied.

"I got a date on Friday night, so if you guys don't mind, I'll take the Pathfinder," Czun replied.

Although the truck belonged to him, he asked out of consideration.

"Fine by me. I'm going out for a few minutes to get some fresh air," Gerald said.

I gave Gerald a nod of acceptance. I knew Gerald was going out to feed, and it made me sad that Gerald chose to endure this burden alone.

Gerald walked outside and looked up at the sky. It was an ideal night for him. The sky was cloudy and overcast, making it a really dark night. The air was still, and the smell of an upcoming rain surrounded him.

Gerald got in his car and turned on the police scanner. He found his potential victim just a few miles up the road. Three men had robbed a liquor store. They held the store clerk and some customers hostage. All Gerald had to do was sneak in, grab the guys, and hopefully, no one got hurt in the prcess.

Gerald arrived at the scene. "Good; they're still here."

Gerald climbed the wall of the adjacent building and leaped 60 feet to the liquor store roof. He listened to the people on the inside and found a spot that was silent. He heard dripping water and a running toilet.

"Sounds like a bathroom," Gerald whispered to himself. Teleporting into the bathroom, Gerald accidentally stepped in the toilet and fell onto the floor. "Awhh- nasty! And that's why I need line of sight to teleport," he said, shaking his wet foot.

"Hey Jeff, go check that out."

"You check it out," the other thief replied.

"Damn cowards," said the third man, walking to the back. "If there is anyone back here, you have three seconds to come out before I start shooting. One-two-three!" The robber shot into the bathroom and kicked the door open only to find no one there. "Must have been a rat. Well, it's gone now!"

The robber turned around the corner; he felt someone touch his shoulder and fainted.

"One down, two to go," Gerald murmured as he teleported through the aisles of the store, purposely bumping over items trying to get the men to separate.

"This is the police—I heard gunshots in there. What's going on in there?" asked the negotiator.

"I have to work fast," Gerald said to himself.

As the two remaining criminals looked out the window toward the police, Gerald ported behind them and drained them.

He ported back to the bathroom, then back to the roof. He began to question himself as he retreated back to his car. "What am I doing? Am I so desperate that I would risk the lives of those people just to feed? I have truly become a monster."

He drove by the scene of the robbery just to see if the victims were all okay. He overheard an old lady say that a dark-skinned angel saved them and that God was watching over them. Those simple words of appreciation renewed Gerald's sense of self-worth.

"What's up yo?" Gerald said as he walked in the door with a smile on his face.

The boys knew that it was Gerald's sign of a good feeding, and they didn't ask about it. Besides, they heard on the police scanner about a dark-skinned angel and figured it was him.

15

Apolice call came through. A man had been murdered and mutilated near Bronze-tone gym on the other side of town.

Gerald stood up. "I was just out that way earlier tonight. I must
have been too weak to pick up on the vibe—sorry, guys."

"There you go blaming yourself again, you can't be everywhere.
Besides, you don't even know when the guy was murdered; or even if
it was a ghoul," said Czun.

"It was, I know it!" Gerald exclaimed.

"Well, let's go get him," I say.

Although we had been on a few adventures together, I had never
seen a ghoul. I was personally interested in seeing if I could communicate with one.

We split up, Czun and I in the Pathfinder and Gerald in the car,
which worked out well because Gerald and I both had telepathy, and
we were learning to talk to each other better. Czun got freaked out at
times; he couldn't stand having someone trying to get into his head.
He had mentioned this to us all the time.

We started a search a few blocks away from the crime scene and
worked our way outward block by block. Then it happened: I got my
first sense of a genuinely undead soul. It was weird, it was wrong, and
it made me nauseous.

"Hey, Gerald, I found one of your homeboys. He's in this old condemned factory building." I spoke out loud so that Czun could hear me verbally and Gerald could hear me telepathically.

"I have been wondering—how is it that you and Gerald are telepathic, but he can teleport, and you can't?" Czun made small talk, noticing my nervousness.

"I was wondering the same thing. I think it may have something to do with the fact that I only have communication to the world of the dead, while Gerald has more of a physical access. And I think that when he teleports, he is actually traveling to the other side and back, and since he is still partially alive, that's why he can only teleport so far, because the longer he's gone, the harder it will be for him to come back. Well, that's what Ty told me anyway. The sad thing is Gerald knows, but he keeps pushing the limit, trying to teleport further and further," I said with a bit of worry in my voice.

I grabbed the machetes from the back and offered one to Czun. Czun looked at me smiled, and flashed his sharp claws and walked toward the building.

"Excuse me, Freddy Krueger!" I said, rolling my head around sarcastically.

They checked the door and found it locked. Then all of a sudden it popped open.

"You weren't going to start without me, were you?" Gerald said as he let us in.

"He's downstairs, and he has company. I can sense five of them," I whispered.

"Yeah and they can sense us like we can sense them, so let's be careful," whispered Gerald.

"Well, they can sense you two but not me—I say you two go ahead, and I will circle behind them, and we will crush them in the middle," Czun said as he tied his hair back.

"You know, that's a really good idea. You ought to be the leader of the gang," Gerald said sarcastically.

"We are a gang now? You guys didn't tell me we were a gang," I said, totally clueless about the joke.

"That's because you aren't part of it," Czun growled as he morphed to his battle mode.

"You can be really mean sometimes," I said as I looked down to unsheathe the machete. "How do you plan to get around behind them without them knowing?" I asked, but when I looked back up, Czun was already gone. "Man, he's fast; I wonder which was faster—his running or your teleporting?"

"That's a good question. I have wondered that myself," laughed Gerald.

Gerald and I headed toward the stairs together. There was a certain aura that circled us when we were together, like we were royalty. I guess we were Princes of the Dead, so to speak. As we got closer to what we figured was surely a trap, we started to breathe shallower and cling to the shadows of the stairwell. We reached the bottom and felt the strong sense of death.

"I have never felt a ghoul this strong—he must be an original, but I thought I killed them all" whispered Gerald.

"You took long enough, boy. Come give your Aunt Helen a kiss," said the ghoul.

"No—you can't be alive!" Gerald gasped.

"Oh, I am very much alive. You should have made sure the knife went all the way through. Instead, it stuck in the floor at an angle, leaving my neck partially attached. It took a long while, but I made it back with the help of someone you may know, little Grey," Helen said with a grin.

"How do you know my name?" I asked.

"I know all about you and your life, and tada—your girlfriend." Helen pointed off to the corner and showed Dawn tied to a bench surrounded by ghouls ready to tear her apart in a mass feeding frenzy.

"All you have to do to keep her alive is—" Helen was cut off by another voice in the background.

"Give your soul to me!" shouted Nyhte.

"Do you know this guy?" asked Gerald, getting into his fighting stance.

"Yeah, this is sort of a family reunion for us, I guess. He's my father," I said with disgust.

"I know there are three of you. So, I will tell you what I'll do. I'll bring out my other surprise, and you come out—okay, Czun?" requested Nyhte as he stretched forth his hands and Xavier's body walked forth. "As you can see, your father is one of my servants, forever, or at least until he decays and falls apart. The choice is yours. All I want is my son, and you all can go back to whatever two bastard kids do without parents."

Nyhte paused for Czun's answer. "Okay, I'll tell you what, I'll let you keep your father. As for you, Gerald, your aunt can't wait to put her arms around you."

"I don't think I am strong enough to take him; he's my father," I said to Gerald telepathically.

"You damn right you can't take me, boy, but I'm glad you are developing the skill of the black art," Nyhte spoke out aloud. "You have one minute to kneel before me, my son."

Gerald and I were frozen in the moment; neither of us knew what to do. But we knew that surrendering wasn't an option. We also knew we were outmatched. Suddenly there was a thunderous roar in the distance, and a ghoul's head rolled across the floor. We looked down at the head as it rolled. Then a loud shrieking squeal came from the corner. Another ghoul shouted out in pain. We looked over and saw his arm was ripped off from the shoulder; the girl it was watching was gone.

Gerald and I moved in for the attack, and Gerald raced toward his aunt.

"You found a cure, I see; too bad it was too little too late." Helen laughed.

"The only thing that is too late is my desire to let you live. You are not the woman I knew," yelled Gerald, trying to convince himself more than anything.

Gerald swung his sword at Helen, but she blocked it.

"I figure I owe you a haircut—remember this machete?" Helen said, blocking Gerald's every attack.

I think she might be too strong for me, Gerald thought.

"Yes, you're right; I am too strong for you—boy." Helen laughed as she sliced at her once-beloved nephew.

I tried to focus my attention. I began to walk up to the man I once called father, preparing to put an end to my fears once and for all.

"I can't believe it; you actually think you can beat me!" laughed Nyhte.

"Wrong answer. I know you can read minds, and all I am thinking of is what time I am going to go to the movies with Dawn after all this is over and done with." I smirked sarcastically.

"You have a fighting spirit like your mother. I broke it too," laughed Nyhte

I took a swing at Nyhte with my machete. Nyhte stuck up his arm in defense and let the machete stick in his arm. Nyhte spun around, knocking me to the floor. Nyhte pulled the knife from his arm; his wounds healed instantly. "You were weak and girlish then, and now you are still a punk. Your weakness comes from your mother's side, obviously!" said Nyhte as he grabbed me by the throat and lifted me in the air.

Another loud roar echoed through the building, and the head of another ghoul rolled across the floor. Another ghoul screamed out in agony.

"I see your friend has killed another of those pathetic ghouls. No matter; you are what I am here for. Legion, arise!" Nyhte commanded, holding out his free hand. A small army of ghouls and undead stormed the room at his command.

Czun somersaulted to the center of the room, morphed back to human form, winked at me, and morphed back, sort of mocking Nyhte and reassuring me everything would be okay.

I looked over at him. I kicked Nyhte between the legs and backed up to Czun's side. "Took you long enough—where were you?"

"I had to wait until the ghouls weren't looking at the girl to make my move, or they would have killed her before I reached her. Where did Gerald go?" Czun asked.

"I don't know; he was right over there with the ghoul he said was his aunt," I replied.

Czun cased around; he noticed that the ghouls and zombies were different from the others he and Gerald had killed before. "These seem to move much quicker than any I have encountered before."

"Do you like my new concoction of creatures of the dark realm, my son? Their only reason for living is to bring you to me so that they can rest in peace." Nyhte laughed sadistically. "I sped up their animation and increased their strength just for you, Czun."

"And what special talent do they have for me?" said Gerald as he appeared beside the closest ghoul to the boys and chopped off its head.

"Quite impressive. I was sure you would be fighting longer or be dead by now. Again, no matter—you will die now anyway. Kill them and bring me my son." Nyhte waved his hand, and the battle began.

Czun and Gerald were literally overcome, but they held their own. I, on the other hand, was taking a severe beating. Czun tried to help me, but there were just too many.

Czun was almost a full werewolf; he wouldn't change all the way for fear he would hurt one of us by accident. Gerald was wearing down; he was growing hungry for essence and ghouls didn't have any he could feed off of. He wouldn't risk weakening Czun to feed. I was on the floor unconscious and still being beaten. The ghouls knew that my soul could be retrieved by Nyhte later. Czun and Gerald were taking some powerful blows from the fiendish dead. Although they fought with all their might, it wasn't enough. They would fight with their last ounce of breath. In a few moments, that point would arrive.

Everything was black; I felt the cold chill of nothingness. I heard a voice of power; it soothed me, it made me strong, then it woke me.

"My turn!" I said from beneath the pile of ghouls.

Ghouls went flying through the air. I stood there with a ghoul by the neck. I felt the heat from an electric charge come from deep inside my body. It coursed through my hand, frying the ghoul I was holding. I cocked my arm back and hurled the sizzling ghoul in Gerald's direction, knocking over a few of Gerald's attackers. A bolt of lightning shot from my hand and revitalized Gerald.

"I am the sovereign of the damned and ruler of lost souls—none shall defy me!" I said, my eyes fixed and focused on my father.

The battle continued. Gerald aided Czun, and they battled side by side. I was on an amazing journey; my destination was across the room to my father. Ghouls and fiends came at me from all direction. I continued, frying them all as I marched forward. My strength and telekinesis were amplified. I started to draw ghouls and fiends toward me and away from my friends so that I could destroy them. Their screams of pain and terror were like music to my ears.

21

"Father, I have a message from Saban—it's time for you to come home!" I said as I approached him.

"You lie; you could never possess the power to visit Saban and return," Nyhte said, a little doubtful of his words.

"Oh, you want proof? No problem." I looked at the ghouls and undead and commanded them. "All ye lost spirits and damned souls, bow down before your prince."

Suddenly the ghouls and undead stopped fighting and bowed down.

"You will die!" Nyhte screamed as he drove a dagger into my heart.

"No, Father, you will die," I demanded as I pulled the knife from my chest and stabbed it into his.

Nyhte fell to the floor. "You are stronger than I imagined; we could have ruled the world together."

"Like you said, I'm just like my mother," I replied as I let my father's body fall to the floor. "As for you lost souls, let his black spirit lead you to the realm of the dead where you belong." With a wave of the hand, Nyhte's spirit rose from his body and disappeared into a shadow on the floor. The other souls followed into a vortex of darkness, and their bodies disintegrated. Xavier waved goodbye to Czun as if to say sorry and thanks as one gesture.

I met Czun and Gerald in the center of the room and headed for the door.

"Sirens—Dawn must have called the cops. Our cover was blown. Forget school; we might get run out of town or worse, lynched," Czun said in a worried overtone

"She's in one of the cop cars. I can read her mind. She's scared to death of you, Czun, but she doesn't know who you really are. I'm going to put a message in her head to forget all names and faces that she saw here," I said with a new sense of confidence.

"Cool. Let's go home; I'm exhausted. What a way to spend a school night," said Gerald.

"Okay, but first I want to know how you killed Helen so quickly?" I asked.

"You can sense that I didn't kill her, I know. I had a choice to either get revenge or back up my brothers. I chose my brothers," Gerald said, putting his head down in failure.

"You did all right by me—sacrifices are what bonds a family together," said Czun as he got in the truck.

We were on our way home. We didn't talk much about what happened that night. It was really tough on us losing our family again after all this time, but as long as we had each other, we would survive.

"Which brings us to you, Lilly. I felt the power of the dark and followed it here. I was surprised to learn that vampires really do exist," Grey said, finishing his story. "Gerald, how did you get here first?"

22

"Well, funny story. I saw a big guy dressed in all black. He was following Lilly. I thought he was going to kidnap or rob her. So, I gave him a touch; nothing happened. He had no essence, and I knew immediately he was a ghoul. We faced off; I tried to explain. He attacked, and I took him out. Lilly saw what happened, and we began to talk. I didn't read her mind. I wanted to learn about her the old-fashioned way. So, I guess we both have our secrets. Well, until tonight." Gerald smiled.

"Gerald's got a girlfriend, Gerald's got a girlfriend," Czun sang out through the telepathic link.

Zarian spoke up. The jealousy was evident in his voice. "My friend has many friends. She likes us the same."

Lilly felt the supernatural testosterone building. "Okay, fellas, it's been real. It's late, and I need to get some sleep. This mind thing is exhausting."

"Yes, time for you to leave." Zarian motioned Gerald toward the door.

"Um, y'all means you too." Lilly pointed at Zarian. "Come back tomorrow night after eight. I got thangs to do. You have already turned my life upside down. I need a minute to evaluate my priorities."

"Okay, my friend. I will see you tomorrow." Zarian bowed. He then stepped forward into nothing and disappeared.

"Wow, that was cool," Gerald said. "I disconnected our telepathic links. We can talk now."

Lilly held up a hand. "What part of y'all don't you people understand?"

Gerald stood up, gave a polite bow, stepped backward, and disappeared.

He reappeared on the roof across the street beside Czun.

"Show-off," Gerald said from down below, looking up at his brothers.

"Grey, did you see where that guy went?" Gerald said through a telepathic link but spoke aloud for Czun to hear.

"He left," Grey replied.

"I know. Where did he go?" Gerald said, losing his patience.

"I mean, he left-left," Grey tried to explain. "He went away completely. When you teleport, there is a trace of you from here to there. He was just gone. Like he stepped out of existence."

"Looks like we got a mystery, Shaggy." Czun morphed his face into a wolf and tried to speak like Scooby-Doo.

CPSIA information can be obtained
at www.ICGtesting.com
Printed in the USA
FSHW011009070919
61778FS